THE EVER

CW00602244

After a shattered romance, the last thing Alix wanted was another man around, least of all somebody as arrogant and domineering as Quinn Tennant. But she had little say in the matter—for Quinn was everywhere! Everywhere but the one place she quickly came to want him: in her heart.

Books you will enjoy
by VICTORIA GORDON

WOLF AT THE DOOR

When Kelly Barnes's father was taken ill, she
knew she was quite capable of standing in for
him for the time being as administrator and cook
at a boom-town camp high up in the Rocky
Mountains. But the camp boss, Grey Scofield,
didn't agree—and so began a battle of wills that
it seemed neither of them would win. Yet *someone*
had to win . . .

THE SUGAR DRAGON

When Verna moved to the Queensland sugar
city of Bundaberg to edit the local newspaper,
she thought she was leaving all her romantic problems behind her—until she met the forceful Con
Bradley, who nicknamed her 'Dragon Lady the
Editor' and turned her world upside down. All of
which was quite enough for Verna to cope with,
even before Madeline Cunningham arrived, with
wedding bells in mind!

THE EVERYWHERE MAN

BY
VICTORIA GORDON

MILLS & BOON LIMITED
15-16 BROOK'S MEWS
LONDON W1A 1DR

All the characters in this book have no existence outside the imagination of the Author, and have no relation whatsoever to anyone bearing the same name or names. They are not even distantly inspired by any individual known or unknown to the Author, and all the incidents are pure invention.

The text of this publication or any part thereof may not be reproduced or transmitted in any form or by any means, electronic or mechanical, including photocopying, recording, storage in an information retrieval system, or otherwise, without the written permission of the publisher.

This book is sold subject to the condition that it shall not, by way of trade or otherwise, be lent, resold, hired out or otherwise circulated without the prior consent of the publisher in any form of binding or cover other than that in which it is published and without a similar condition including this condition being imposed on the subsequent purchaser.

First published 1981
Australian copyright 1981
Philippine copyright 1981
This edition 1981

© Victoria Gordon 1981

ISBN 0 263 73598 2

Set in Monophoto Baskerville 10 on 10½ pt.

Made and printed in Great Britain by
Richard Clay (The Chaucer Press) Ltd,
Bungay, Suffolk

This book owes much to Vivian Smith and Leni McKenzie, who are the heart and soul of the Bundaberg Obedience Dog Club.

CHAPTER ONE

IT was the sound that woke her. A strange, eerie sound that began like a soft wind, whispering secrets to the high leaves of the gum trees, then deepened, thrusting its voice into a full-throated, bellowing roar that crackled with hidden danger. Bushfire!

No one who had spent a lifetime in south-central Victoria could mistake that sound. Certainly not a girl who had lost both parents to a raging bushfire only five years before. Alix snapped erect, ignoring the spasm of pain the movement caused in her slender, swan-like neck. Her eyes, a curious yellow-green colour and slanted ever so slightly, sprang open to widen in horror at the rosy hues of the darkening evening sky.

She swung her long legs out of the station sedan, fingers instinctively fumbling for the whistle that hung by a lanyard round her neck.

'Nick! Nick-Nick-Nick!' Her voice snapped out the commanding cry, then she followed up with a long, trilling blast on the whistle. The sound of the fire seemed to mushroom in her ears, surging and roaring like a deadly crimson surf.

'Nick!' She screamed it this time, then sighed with visible relief as the big dog burst from the underbrush and hurtled up to her. He came with that strange, walking-on-glass gait so typical of German Shorthaired Pointers, a high-stepping, ground-covering trot that never ceased to amaze Alix.

But not now! Her neck hurt and her eyes throbbed from the effort of covering nearly two thousand kilometres in two days, and despite her panic, she moved stiffly as she waved the big dog into the rear of the vehicle and slammed the tailgate.

Then she ran for the driver's door, mentally cursing herself for having stopped in this isolated section of scrub in the first place. She was only about thirty-five kilometres from Bundaberg, her destination in the long trek from Melbourne, but her own physical exhaustion and the onset of dusk had combined to cause the halt. Dusk is the absolute worst time of day for driving. Her father had always said so, and Bruce had agreed. It was a time when the eyes played tricks with the light, and a time when too many other drivers took chances by driving without headlights. It was a time when the kangaroos and the wallabies came out to play in the traffic, and Alix had seen once or twice what damage a kangaroo can cause to a car when struck by an unwary driver.

So she had pulled off the road at dusk, just as she had done briefly the evening before, so few hours and so many, many kilometres away, far to the south and west near the Victoria/New South Wales border. Here, in south-eastern Queensland, dusk came a shade earlier, but she could probably have made it to Bundaberg before full dark. It was only for her own peace of mind, and to give Nick some much-needed exercise, that she had stopped. And now . . .

The wheels of the station sedan sprayed up a cloud of dirt and leaves and broken twigs as she slammed it into gear and slewed down the narrow scrub track to the highway.

She shot out on to the bitumen before she realised it was there, and she spun the steering wheel and snapped on her headlights as she fought to keep the heavy machine on the road. The rear end skidded, throwing the front over to the wrong side of the road just as Alix suddenly realised there was another set of headlights speeding towards her. She swung into the skid as the other driver swung away from her, and then there was a moment when she was certain they would strike head-on. But somehow he missed her, and the relief cost her the last shred of her concentration. The station sedan slithered into the ditch and came to rest in the long grass and rubble.

Instinct and half-forgotten driver training made Alix flick off the ignition before she threw her arms across the steering wheel and bowed her head as tears sprang to her eyes and great, convulsive sobs shook her slender frame. In the rear, Nick whimpered in confused sympathy, a whimper that suddenly changed to a growl as Alix's door was flung open and a hand reached in to grasp the shoulder of her jumper and drag her out of the vehicle.

'Are you drunk, or crazy, or what?' a voice grated in livid rage. And then, only a shade less angrily, 'Are you all right?'

'I'm . . . fine,' she whispered, unable to quell the shaking of her body as reaction took over. She was trembling like a leaf as strong hands closed around her shoulders just before she collapsed.

She returned to consciousness disorientated, and her confusion changed to outright fear as she opened her eyes and found herself being held, almost like a baby, in the arms of a man she had never seen before.

'Ssshhh! It's all right,' growled a strangely gentle voice, and the arms which held her across his lap relaxed slightly, as if to assure her she wasn't being held against her will.

Alix shook her head, only vaguely aware that the movement loosened the high-piled knot of hair at her crown, letting it spill down in a shower of chestnut across his arm. Then memory, or a semblance of it, returned.

'N-Nick?' she cried softly, eyes probing his face for an answer she feared.

'The dog? He's all right. I'd have let him out, but I reckoned he might decide to take my arm off or something. But you? Are you all right now?'

Eyes like sparkling diamonds, only a clear, dark grass green, bored into hers as he shifted his arm so that Alix could straighten up. She could see, then, that they were in the front of what she presumed must be his vehicle, parked nose into the narrow track from which she had emerged so precipitously only moments—hours?—before.

'Here. I reckon we could both use this.' She turned to look at him again, barely aware of the flask he was holding out to her. 'It's only brandy; it won't hurt you,' he said, and she took it without another thought.

The stranger took a deep swallow of the liquor himself, strong throat muscles flexing with the movement. He looked at Alix again as if reassuring himself that she was fit to be questioned, and when he spoke again there was less gentleness in his voice.

'Now maybe you can explain just what the hell you were trying to do back there,' he said. 'You came awful damned close to killing us both, in case you don't realise it. What's the idea of screaming out of the scrub like that with no lights on and without even stopping to look for traffic?'

The liquor eased a warm track down Alix's throat to puddle in a fiery pool in her tummy, and the warmth brought back old terrors. Her eyes widened and she snapped her head around in a revealingly fearful motion.

'The . . . the fire!' she whispered, suddenly confused by what she couldn't see. Around them was only darkness, broken by the cast of his parking lights against the track ahead and by the dying breath of twilight against the trees to her right. But of the fire, the sky-painting crimson wash that had panicked her—there wasn't a sign. 'B-b-bushfire,' she stammered in a whimper of frightened disbelief.

'Bushfire? There was no bushfire,' he growled. 'They were just firing some cane up the road there. Do you mean to tell me *that*'s what scared you?'

The disbelief and . . . was it contempt? . . . in his eyes brought Alix upright as anger purged the confusion from her brain.

'Well, of course I was frightened!' she snarled, thrusting away his arm as she struggled to shift herself totally away from him. The look of half-amused contempt on his face infuriated Alix more than her own fears shamed her. Maybe she should have recognised the cane fire, although just how she might be expected to, she didn't know. She had never seen sugarcane being fired, but she had read up enough on the industry and the Bundaberg region to know the cane harvest would be in full swing by the time she got there.

She *knew* that the trash of useless cane leaves and foliage was burned both to destroy the snakes and insects harboured there and to raise the sugar in the stalks of cane, and she *knew* that the firing created a holocaust that flared and died within minutes, but knowledge from a book could do nothing to prepare her for the horrifying fear that an unexpected cane fire could produce inside her.

And now here was this . . . this arrogant, sneering man, who dared to smirk at her fears.

'Well, I'm glad you think it's so damned funny,' she snapped, swinging her legs out the open door of the Range Rover. But before they could touch the ground a hand flashed out to grasp her shoulder and pull her back inside.

'I never said it was funny,' he replied with exasperating calmness. 'Now just settle down, because you're not going anywhere in that state. You may be too angry to realise it, but you're in shock, my girl.'

'I am *not* your girl!' Alix retorted angrily, pushing away his hand and in the same motion rejecting the brandy flask he was once again offering. 'Nor anyone else's, either. And I don't *want* any more of your damned brandy.'

'Just as well you aren't *my girl*,' he replied, 'or you'd be over my knee getting your pretty little rump paddled. Now settle down! And for once try acting your age; you're not a child.'

'I'm surprised you'd notice,' she snapped, retreating to the very edge of her seat. 'And just who do you think you are—telling me what I can do and what I can't?'

'I'm the man you damned near ran off the road with your damned-fool driving,' he replied with growing anger. 'So the least you can do, since you don't seem to even have thought of apologising, is explain to me what you were doing back in here in the first place.'

'Well, what do you think?' she replied in a tone of voice that implied he should imagine it was a comfort stop and that he'd be wrong.

He didn't bother to reply, and when Alix turned to face him squarely she could see that he wasn't about to. His fiery green eyes were blank with determined stubbornness, and that same stubbornness was stamped on every feature of his face.

A rather handsome face it was too, she couldn't help thinking. A strong chin, wide, determined, but generous mouth, slightly crooked nose and heavy, sloping eyebrows. Laugh wrinkles round the eyes and worry wrinkles on his forehead, coffee-coloured hair a little too long to be classically stylish.

But it was his eyes that commanded the attention. Where Alix had slanted, oval eyes beneath straight, up-swept brows that made them seem wide and highlighted their yellow-green colour, this man's eyes were small and deep-set. Not piggy-small, but so deep beneath his heavy brows and partially hidden by folds of eyelid that they *seemed* small. And bright! Bright like a green fire, like smouldering emeralds or grass-green diamonds, because surely no emerald could flash like that.

A strong, muscular neck led her eyes to a broad chest with a thatch of coffee hair protruding from the half-open front of his drill shirt, and the legs beneath the drill trousers were obviously well muscled and sturdy. He'd be tall, she thought, perhaps six foot and probably an inch or so over that. On the ground he would have towered above her slender five foot nine, but here in the vehicle the difference was less apparent.

Handsome, definitely. But so arrogant. And despite the tangled, shaggy hair that showed not a hint of grey, he'd be ... thirty-five ... probably closer to forty. Shirt-sleeves rolled up along muscular forearms ... good, strong, well-shaped hands ... clean fingernails, not manicured, but tidy ...

Alix suddenly realised she had been assessing this stran-ger for far longer than propriety or common sense would allow, and that he was not unaware of her assessment. His eyes seemed to twinkle at her sudden start of confu-sion.

'Well, if you must know, I was ... resting,' she replied with tongue-tying haste. 'And exercising the dog.'

'Not very bright,' he murmured almost to himself, but Alix caught the words.

'What did you say?' He couldn't have said that, she thought. I must have misunderstood.

'I said it wasn't very bright,' he replied with increasing volume, and this time there was no mistake.

'I don't think I know what you mean,' she replied cauti-ously.

'Obviously,' he replied with a taut little twist of his generous lower lip. And then sat in silence, his eyes roving over Alix as if she were some unusual museum specimen and a rather unwholesome one at that.

'Well, then perhaps you'd like to explain,' she said, not bothering to try and hide her exasperation.

His hand made a gesture of obvious disgust. 'You really think it's smart to be running your dog in a patch of strange scrub, in questionable light, only fifty feet from a main highway? What if he'd jumped a hare or something and chased it out on to the road? One dog—and a valuable dog, from the look of him—splattered all over the road because you're too lazy to walk him on a leash.'

'And who said he wasn't on a leash?' Alix felt the warm glow rising up her throat that announced the lie she was implying, and she knew instantly that she wasn't fooling anyone. Her inquisitor merely raised one eyebrow and quirked the corner of his mouth as she stumbled on. 'And besides, he doesn't chase rabbits . . .'

She didn't bother to finish that statement. The look on his face was that of a stern headmaster faced with a recalcitrant student who should know better. 'I've seen older and wiser G.S.P.s than that one get hurt doing exactly what I just described,' he said wearily, revealing by his use of the initials that he wasn't unfamiliar with German Shorthaired Pointers. Among dog fanciers, the unwieldy name was invariably shortened to the three initials, and his use of them implied a familiarity Alix would rather not have known.

Her dog was of a breed whose popularity, though increasing, fought a continuous battle, because the dogs had a well-founded reputation for stubborn independence. Gundog fanciers tended to either love them—hence owning them—or hated them with an almost fanatical dislike that far outweighed the preference for more conventional breeds. And although Nick was among the most faithful and generally obedient of dogs, his independent spirit required constant surveillance to keep him from getting out of hand.

He might very well have chased himself into danger, and the acceptance of her responsibility for Nick's safety brought Alix down out of her anger.

'You're right,' she admitted lamely. 'If it's any real con-solation, I don't generally do things like that, either, but . . .'

'Doesn't matter now,' he interrupted. 'I wasn't trying to tell you how to lead your life, just keep you talking until I could be sure you were getting back to normal.'

The sudden switch to an apparent total indifference both confused and surprised Alix, but before she could reply he was out of the vehicle and coming round to help her step down as well.

'Let's just see if you're as steady with your feet as you should be,' he said, steadying her as she swung down on to the ground. Standing, he was even taller than Alix had thought, a least six foot three, and his hand on her upper arm had the strength of an iron clamp.

'I'm fine,' she said, shrugging against his grasp, but he ignored her, and didn't remove his hand until she had walked several steps in her attempts to free herself. Looking up at him, she found the rising moon cast an almost satanic light on his features, and suddenly she wanted nothing more than to get back into her station sedan and get away from him.

'If you'd like to go and get in the wagon, then, we'll see if we can't do something about getting you back on the road,' he muttered, stepping back into his Range Rover in one smooth gesture almost as he spoke. He put on the headlights and backed cautiously out on to the highway, leaving Alix to walk in sudden comparative darkness to fumble her way into the ditch to the door of her station sedan.

Nick whined a greeting from the rear, scrabbling at the wire netting which separated him from the passenger com-partment and vocalising his discontent until Alix snapped at him to be quiet.

She sat in silence, mildly piqued by the stranger's entire attitude, as he used the lights of his vehicle and a small torch to evaluate her position. Then, somewhat to her surprise, he drove the Range Rover down into the ditch and around her, stopping just in front before he emerged carrying a length of sturdy rope.

'You might come and hold this light for me,' he said, dropping to his knees in front of her vehicle, but even before Alix had scrambled out and reached for the torch, he had fastened one end of the rope and was lifting himself erect again.

'Right! The best way is for me to drag you straight up the ditch there to where it isn't quite so steep,' he said. 'Now I don't want you to try and help—just leave it in neutral and let the Rover do the work.'

'But surely . . .' She had intended to suggest that the power of her vehicle would take some of the strain from his, but he interrupted her almost angrily.

'Surely nothing! My way, everything will be done under control. You start interfering and you might come up out of that ditch too fast to maintain control. And we've already seen what happens when you lose control—remember?'

Alix bristled at the remark, but to no avail. He didn't even notice, having walked away to attach the other end of the rope to the trailer hitch on his Rover. She got back into her wagon as he slowly eased forward, taking up the strain gently so that the elasticity in the nylon rope wouldn't cause her vehicle to suddenly surge ahead.

The rope seemed to stretch forever before suddenly her car began to spring forward, and Alix touched gently at the brake to keep from moving too quickly. They moved up the ditch for several metres before he aimed his Rover at the slope, where it clawed its way up on a frightening angle. When Alix's wagon reached the incline, dangling almost like a pendulum, it slid alarmingly sideways before suddenly thrusting up over the crest and across the highway to come to a halt behind the Rover.

'Nothing to it,' the tall man grinned as he slid from his vehicle and began disengaging the tow-rope. He coiled the rope and flung it carelessly into the rear compartment of the Rover, then abruptly ordered Alix to open the bonnet of her own vehicle.

There was just enough arrogance in the gesture that she immediately bristled, questioning out loud the need for such action.

'Well, just for starters I'd like to make sure you haven't

punched a hole in the radiator or some such thing,' he retorted coolly. 'Cars like this aren't exactly designed for driving down ditches, you know.'

Flushing with the impact of his implied criticism, Alix pulled the appropriate lever and then went to stand beside him as he used the torch to inspect the innards of her wagon. It took him only a few minutes, but they stretched out as he mumbled to himself throughout the exercise.

'Looks all right,' he finally muttered in grudging tones. 'Now we'll just have a final check on His Majesty here, and then you can go back to being the terror of the highways again.'

Alix squeaked out a protest that the stranger blithely ignored as he reached into her vehicle for the leash and chain collar that lay on the passenger seat. Striding confidently to the rear of the station wagon, he flung open the tailgate and said, 'All right, old Nick. Come out of there and let's have a look at you.'

Somewhat to Alix's chagrin, Nick bounced down, his stub of a tail fluttering vigorously as the tall man slipped the collar over his head and led him at a brisk trot along the shoulder of the highway. The man's easy handling of the dog bespoke a long familiarity with dogs, but even so, Alix couldn't quite understand the ease with which Nick accepted him. The big dog had been hers since he was a puppy, and normally was both reserved and stand-offish with strangers.

'All right, back you go,' said the man, and Nick hopped obediently into the rear of the vehicle, sitting patiently as the collar and lead were removed. He didn't even whimper as the tail-gate was closed upon him; just sat in quiet observation as the man turned and handed the leash back to Alix.

'He moves well,' he said, and Alix could only nod at the compliment before the voice continued, 'You're sure you feel all right to drive now? It's not that far to Bundy in any event, but I'll stick around if you'd rather sit a bit longer.'

'I'm just fine,' she replied, 'and in any event I hardly think I need a nursemaid.'

She regretted the provocative remark even as it passed

her lips, but once said it couldn't be retracted, and she stood looking defiantly up at his faintly amused grin.

'Well, if you'd had a better one when you were a child you might show better manners,' he said then. 'Or is it part of some Women's Lib programme to be ungrateful, stroppy and generally disagreeable?'

'Well, what would you like me to do—get down and kiss your feet?' she retorted angrily. 'I'm afraid that's too high a price just for a little tow out of the ditch, if you don't mind.'

'Actually, a simple thank you would have sufficed,' he replied grimly. 'We'll just ignore the possibility of you saying you're sorry for damned near killing us both with your stupid driving.'

'All right! Thank you. And I'm sorry for driving so poorly and I'm sorry I almost ran you off the road. Are you happy now?' The words emerged in an atmosphere so chilly Alix almost expected to see them solid in the air between them, sheathed in ice. And she didn't care, either. This man's absurd arrogance was just a little too much to bear after two long days of driving.

He shook his head sadly. 'Childishness doesn't become you, despite your tender years,' he said quietly, but scorn was evident in his eyes.

'I'm twenty-seven years old, not that it's any of your business,' Alix retorted hotly.

'Well, fancy that! I'd have said more like ten or twelve,' he replied. 'But I'll take your word for it, although thousands wouldn't.'

'Which doesn't concern me in the slightest,' she answered, shaking her head in a haughty gesture that sent her hair flying round her head in a shimmering halo. Damn the man, anyway. He was deliberately baiting her, and she didn't seem capable of avoiding the verbal traps he was setting with every comment.

Alix turned away, walking to the driver's door of her vehicle in total awareness of the tall figure by her side. She opened the door and flung the leash and collar inside with a gesture that revealed more of her anger than she would normally have wished.

'You've been very kind, I suppose,' she said with what she hoped was total calm. 'I think I'll go now.'

'But you haven't kissed my feet yet,' he said so quietly she barely heard him. Yet not too quietly, and Alix couldn't help the reflex that spun her round to face him once again.

'Nor shall I . . .' she began, only to find herself being pulled toward him, her shoulders imprisoned by strong hands as his lips bent to meet her own.

The kiss was far from gentle, yet it held no crude savagery. Only a vast *knowing*, a deliberate and experienced expertise that somehow swept aside her surprise and anger so that she was responding before she realised it. His lips claimed her mouth and the hard length of his body was startlingly aware of her own slender figure as some intangible current sparked between them.

It went on and on, one of his hands dropping from her shoulder to hold her even closer against him as he explored her mouth with his own until finally Alix's inner strength took hold once again.

Her free hand slashed towards his face, claws outstretched as she struggled to draw her face away from his tauntingly knowledgeable lips, but he reached up to catch her wrist in mid-air and the grin on his face said almost everything. Almost . . .

'Naughty, naughty,' he chuckled, and stood there, a look of quiet, dominating amusement in his fire-green eyes as Alix struggled in futile rage to free herself.

'You . . . you . . .!' Words failed her; she could only stare up at him, vainly hoping that looks could kill.

'Try *bastard*,' he grinned. 'It's true, too, at least in its proper usage. And I'll take back what I said earlier—you're a little older than twelve.'

'You're contemptible!'

'No. I just believe in paying my debts, and in having debts paid to me as they're owed,' he replied, still making no move towards releasing her.

Alix tensed, raising one foot as the thought of kicking him occurred to her, but he raised one eyebrow in reproach and warned her against it. 'I'd only kick you back, if nothing else,' he laughed. 'Why not relax? You've only one more kiss to finish the debt.'

And he'd have it, too. Alix knew her strength was no match for this tall, powerful stranger. Strangely, she felt no great fear of him. He wasn't a rapist or a madman, just a strong, self-assured and terribly masculine person who would have his own way in this disagreement but would never really harm her. How did she know that? she wondered. How *could* she? Yet she did, though it wasn't quite the comforting thought it might have been.

'I think perhaps you over-value yourself,' she replied, stiffly holding herself away from him and trying to ignore the helplessness she felt.

'Now that's something I never do,' he said calmly.

'So you're conceited as well!'

'Only last year; this year I'm perfect,' he replied quite soberly, but the laughter was there, in those mocking green eyes, and Alix couldn't quite repress a chuckle of her own at the hoary old line.

'Has it occurred to you that perhaps I simply don't *want* to kiss you again?' she said, trying to get some lightness into her voice.

'Oh, indeed. But you will, because you're an honourable woman, all else aside,' he said. 'I'm sure you also believe in paying your debts.'

'I didn't contract any debt with you,' said Alix.

'Well, we could always push your car back into the ditch,' he said. 'That way you wouldn't have to kiss me again. We'd be even for you having run me off the road, and . . .'

'And you don't know how tempting a suggestion that is,' she interrupted. 'Personally I'd rather just get it over with.' And she stood there, eyes closed and lips pursed as she waited, looking like a sulky, spoiled child and all too well aware of it.

His fingers tightened on her shoulder, but only for an instant, and then—even with her eyes shut—she knew he had moved away from her. The removal of his hands was like the breaking of an unseen current.

It was a trick! But even as she thought it, Alix knew she

was mistaken, and the proof was there when she finally worked up the nerve to open her eyes. He was gone, walking back towards his Rover without a backward glance.

'But . . .' she whispered the word unconsciously, hardly expecting, once it had escaped, that he might have heard her. But of course he would . . . and he did.

'I'll take a rain check,' he replied without looking back, and the words floated back to her with a tangible amusement that nearly made her stamp one foot in renewed anger. Then his truck door slammed and the engine rumbled to life as he swung into a U-turn that returned him to his original direction. And he drove past her with a mocking grin and a superior thumbs-up gesture that was almost defiant.

Alix returned the gesture halfheartedly, then grinned to herself as she settled into her own vehicle and reached to fasten the seat belt. By the time she was half a kilometre down the road, the humour of the entire situation had her chuckling aloud, amused as much at her own come-uppance—well deserved—as anything else.

What a fiasco. And what a man! Even with his arrogance and high-handed, masculine superiority, she had to admit he had broken off the encounter—deliberately—at a point where neither of them suffered any severe loss of face. A second kiss would have been a less satisfactory conclusion for her, she admitted, and he had lost nothing by taking his 'rain check'—except for the likelihood of ever collecting on it.

He didn't even know her name. Not that it mattered, of course, since she couldn't imagine their paths crossing anyway. Unless, perhaps, he was from Bundaberg. But he'd been going *away* from the sugar city, and late enough at night that she might reasonably expect him to be on his way home.

During the next few moments she couldn't help wondering about him, though. Especially by comparison to Bruce, and that didn't please Alix very much at all.

Bruce! Damn Bruce anyway. Damn Bruce and damn all men, she thought, responding instinctively to the hurt that welled up inside her as she thought of her handsome Canadian fiancé—former fiancé—who had jilted her in a fashion so chillingly, horribly final that she still had trouble comprehending it.

Bruce had been an architect, and a good one. His position with the firm she had worked for in Melbourne was part of an exchange programme with a Canadian branch of the firm, and almost from the first day he had arrived—two years before—Alix had found their attraction both mutual and gratifying.

Tall, blond and so handsome he was almost pretty, Bruce had been the object of intense attention from every female in the firm. Alix had been no less intrigued than the other girls, but she had had the advantage of being chosen to work closely with him on the first of many important jobs where her talents as a design draughtswoman played a significant role.

Within a week he had asked her to dinner; within a month they were constantly in each other's company. By the end of the first year they were making serious plans for marriage—or at least Alix thought they were serious.

How could she have been so naïve? So blind? Even in retrospect—especially in retrospect—she could see that all of the plans and dreams were centred on one thing: Bruce's eventual return to Canada was a preface to all of their planning.

Thinking of it now, Alix realised that he had hated Australia, covering his hatred with a veneer of amused contempt that she had often found just a trifle hard to bear. Except that she had loved him, and therefore been able to gloss over his deficiencies to keep him high and unsullied on the pedestal in her heart.

And he had been so suave, so gentle and forgiving and non-aggressive in his lovemaking. He had never questioned Alix's rather inexperienced shyness, never wondered that she had come to the age of twenty-five with firm if somewhat old-fashioned ideas about premarital sex. Indeed, he had accepted it a shade too readily, she reflected, and realised she had often thought him just a shade too patient in his approaches.

Too patient! What a laugh that was now. Of course he

had been patient; it wasn't difficult for somebody involved not in love, not in planning for a life together at all, but only playing a cunning, deceitful game that cleverly covered up his real interests.

It hadn't been until he had gone—returned to Canada on an aircraft at exactly the moment she had been waiting for him in *their* favourite little restaurant—that an older, wiser, and maliciously well-meaning co-worker had finally helped Alix to see the truth.

Alix had suffered in silence the first few days of meaningful winks and nudges and pitying glances. In truth she was barely aware of them, suffocating as she was in her own confusion and pain. Bruce gone! Not a word, not a note, not any sort of explanation. Just gone! He had disappeared like the proverbial thief in the night, and not until the following Monday did she receive confirmation that he had actually left the country.

And thief in the night was too good a simile, she found out much, much later. Later, when the hurt and pain had begun to scar over, when she had been so gently and so deliberately advised of what he had really been doing on the two nights a week he had always insisted on reserving for 'study'. He had been studying all right, studying a more compliant and willing type of Australian woman than Alix ever intended to be. And that one of them had been her flatmate, a girl living with studied and coldhearted pseudo-innocence beneath the same roof . . .

That had been her only satisfaction in the whole affair—being able to stack Monica's hastily packed luggage on the front porch of the house left to Alix by her parents and icily command the saucy redhead to leave and never, never return. But it was small compensation compared to the announcement in the company newsletter of Bruce's marriage to a childhood sweetheart in Canada, and much, much less than the final galling insult.

The design award he had won—in Canada and while he was still in Australia—was *her* design. Alix's very own work, altered only enough so that he could easily claim credit even if she dared to lodge a complaint.

She hadn't, of course. And he had known she wouldn't,

had counted on it in fact. Nor would she register complaint about the half-dozen other drawings she had found missing from the portfolio she kept of ideas for improving known and patented products that for one reason or another had caught her interest.

Alix, of course, hadn't realised the significance of her improvements. She was no design engineer, no architect. She was merely a draughtswoman and a good one, with an eye for detail, an eye for structure and design and—thanks to Bruce's two 'study' nights each week—the time to doodle away the long hours without him.

Nobody else knew of that particular aspect of her talent, since it wasn't especially called for in her job. She had won a couple of contests and competitions, working and entering them on a freelance basis, but none were of a type to interest her firm and they went unnoticed by everyone but Bruce. Bruce the bastard!

What everyone did notice, however, was how seriously Alix had been rocked by Bruce's abrupt departure. There was an initial hiatus before several other young men in the firm began to make tentative approaches of their own. But it wasn't until her first date with the fourth one in a row to get quite demandingly specific that Alix finally became aware of the final, ultimate degradation. This young man, who had worked quite closely with Bruce, was sufficiently less diplomatic than the others for Alix to finally get the message loud and clear.

She had handled the revelation quite well, she thought. At least on the surface. There was nothing she could do about the scalding tears inside that tore open all of her heart-wounds anew and left them brimming with pain.

'I would have thought you'd worked with Bruce long enough to *know* what a liar he is,' she had told the insistent young man in tones so icily, nonchalantly chilling that he had actually drawn away from her in surprised confusion. It was enough of a foot in the door to give Alix confidence, and she had followed up swiftly.

'Even if I did sleep around,' she had declared, 'it would take far more than a dinner out and an evening at the theatre to give somebody like *you* a hope!' Whereupon she had left him ... simply picked up her purse, opened the door of his shiny new car, and walked slowly and calmly into her yard. She had even paused to pat Nick on the head as he came to greet her at the gate. Not a tear, not a tremble, not a single obvious sign of the demon that raged inside her, frothing to be displayed in tears and tantrums and visible despair.

She had even fooled herself, to some degree. She waited until the offensive young man had driven away, smiled when Nick had trotted over bearing collar and lead, and spent the next two hours exercising him in the safe, silent darkness of a nearby park. It wasn't until she was alone in her bed with the big dog sprawled on the floor beside her that the first tear came.

Then she sobbed and cried all night, with the bewildered G.S.P. whining his own accompaniment as he tried to comfort her without knowing how.

Alix had never been over-superstitious, but she came to think of that night as an omen. It cured her for ever of Bruce, for one thing. But more important, it helped prepare her mind for what happened the next day—for the biggest and best omen of all:

She arrived at work with her resignation already written in her head, and stared only briefly through red-rimmed eyes at the typewriter she borrowed to compose it. No excuses, no reasons, only the bare bones of it. She had enjoyed her work but felt a change was vital to her future. She would prefer to give no notice at all, but would, of course, work out the generally accepted month's notice if required.

It was signed, sealed, and on the General Manager's desk before the G.M. arrived that morning, but only moments before a vaguely confused switchboard operator announced that Alix had a long-distance call. A Mr Jennings from Bundaberg. Did she know him?

Alix did not. Nor, she feared, did her exhausted brain totally comprehend the man's words. He would be in Melbourne two days hence. He wanted to talk to her, to see some more of her work. More? He had a job proposition he thought might interest her—design work, engineering, and then he mentioned the firm for which he was business manager.

After she hung up, Alix wandered the rest of the day in a daze of wonder and surprise. Jennings' firm was a small one, but it had an impressive record for innovative, creative work. And he wanted to offer *her* a job? It was incredible!

She had already decided to accept the job when Mr Jennings arrived in Melbourne and telephoned to confirm their personal meeting. Armed with a portfolio of her best work, along with what remained of the portfolio Bruce had raided, Alix arrived at Mr Jennings' hotel room to find herself confronted by a stout, greying man whose merry, twinkling eyes and friendly smile immediately put her at ease.

He had seen . . . no, his boss had seen . . . Alix's designs in a competition some time earlier. It was one she hadn't placed in, but apparently the boss had been impressed enough to remember her when an opening arose that suited her talents. Would she come to Bundaberg? 'Yes.' Emphatically, enthusiastically yes! The salary was more than agreeable, the type of work was what she had often dreamed of, and of course the timing was perfect, although she didn't enlighten dear Mr Jennings about *that*.

She had worked out her notice in a growing aura of happy anticipation, anticipation that heightened when Mr Jennings wrote to confirm the appointment, to advise that he had found her a place to live with appropriate consideration for Nick, and later with maps and directions and even a travel allowance.

Alix paused on the outskirts of Bundaberg to consult Mr Jennings' map yet again. She had already taken his advice by turning off at Childers on to what he had called the 'Goodwood' road, which brought her into the sugar city by way of Barolin Street, according to the neatly drawn chart. It got trickier once she was in town, but eventually Alix found the proper street and the proper house. For a moment she was awestruck.

CHAPTER TWO

ALIX fell in love with the house at first glance, even knowing that she wouldn't be living in the house itself. It was huge, standing high on stilts in the accredited Queensland 'Colonial' styling. A cunning architect or designer had been at work to restore this former mansion, however, blending modern materials with old-time styling to achieve the best of both periods.

A broad veranda surrounded the structure, and some sections had been screened off to expand the usable space. Some of the windows were stained glass, but others had been fitted with expensive aluminium screening and modern catches to allow total ventilation without accompanying insect visitors.

Underneath the spreading skirts of the house, space had been provided for at least two vehicles. Alix could see the rump of a Citroën CX in one stall, suggesting the owner didn't want for cash, and beside the double driveway another narrow track led past the house itself into the darkened interior of a yard that must have sprawled over a full acre of land, perhaps more.

It was there, Alix knew, that her own 'home' was located, a former gardener's cottage converted by the owner to a private studio and now, apparently, superfluous to his needs. And best of all, according to Mr Jennings' letter, there was a fully-fenced rear yard and proper kennels besides. What a boon for Nick, who had become used to having a yard to run in while Alix was at work each day.

Cautioning the big dog to patience, Alix stepped from the vehicle and then paused on the footpath outside the house. Front door or back? she wondered, suddenly apprehensive about her approach. The decision was made for her when the front porch light burst into life, revealing a tiny, rather stout woman in her sixties scampering down the front staircase with almost fearsome haste.

'You'll be Miss McLean,' the woman twittered breathlessly. 'I'm Mrs Babcock and I'm *so* glad you've arrived safely. I was beginning to worry, what with the dark and all. Now you just take the car round that far track there, my dear, and you'll find yourself right in the cottage carport. I'll walk round and show you the way.'

And she was gone, following her torch beam into the darkness beside the house before Alix could utter a single word. Smothering a wry grin, Alix returned to her car and carefully drove it in as directed, swerving round the corner of the house to find herself facing the grinning maw of a carport and small cottage almost smothered in the flame orange blossoms of Japanese honeysuckle. The huge climbing vine had been carefully manipulated so that it covered the side and roof of the carport and sprawled up over the high-sloped roof of the cottage as well, and the ground beside the cottage was a sea of fallen orange blossoms.

'Here, let me help you, dear.' Mrs Babcock was beside Alix as the car halted, reaching out with a tangible friendliness that Alix couldn't ignore.

The woman's birdlike voice and strong North Queensland accent made her difficult to follow as she chattered on a mile a minute, but the steady flow of conversation relieved Alix of saying anything at all, since Mrs Babcock seemed to be one of those people who answer their own questions.

The only time she paused was when Nick emerged from the rear of the station wagon, bounding through the open gate to begin a thorough inspection of the yard. Head lowered as he sniffed at the ground, his tail flickering like a demented metronome as he trotted curiously around, he totally ignored both women.

'Oh, isn't he a beauty?' Mrs Babcock enthused. 'Oh, my, Anna's going to love him . . . my very word!'

Who 'Anna' might be, she gave no indication, swiftly changing the topic as she chattered on about Alix's trip, and the strain of long-distance driving, and how Alix must be just exhausted. Just keeping up with her was strain enough in Alix's admitted tiredness, but the woman was so

honestly good-natured and concerned that Alix merely
followed her in silence as she produced a key to open the
small cottage.

It faced into the yard and the lushness of the subtropical
growth that surrounded the yard in a protective mantle of
huge ferns, massive, spreading poinciana trees, native
eucalypts and brightly flowering shrubs Alix didn't recognise. It was a small cottage, but from the moment the
door opened she knew it was perfect.

The screened front door opened into a small and yet
spacious   lounge-room-cum-kitchen-cum-dining-room,
where one highlight was a mountain of sandwiches and an
enormous bowl of fresh fruits.

'I was sure you'd need something, and probably be far
too tired to worry about cooking,' said Mrs Babcock. 'Now
you just organise your luggage and have a wee wash while
I put the tea on . . . unless you'd prefer coffee . . . there's
milk in the fridge, anyway, and sugar in this bowl here.
And here in this cupboard there's some fresh bread and
some strawberry jam and marmalade, because of course,
arriving on a Saturday night like this it could be difficult to
get things tomorrow . . .'

Alix lugged her suitcases into the cottage's single bedroom, once again surprised at the space of it. And at
finding the bed already made up with crisp white sheets
and a fluffy comforter. Even a hot water bottle! Goodness,
she thought, I haven't seen a hot water bottle since I was
ten years old.

'I wasn't sure if you'd be bringing your own bedding or
not, and we've plenty to spare in any event,' said Mrs
Babcock from the doorway. 'Come now and have some hot
tea and something to eat. My goodness, child, you look
totally exhausted! Well, I won't stay, only long enough to
be sure you eat something and drink your tea. Not healthy
to bed down on an empty stomach, not after all that driving . . .'

It went on and on, making Alix feel more and more like
the only chick of a broody hen. Closing her eyes, she leaned
back and sipped the tea, not listening, yet calmed by the
chatter.

Momentarily refreshed, she forced herself to eat some of Mrs Babcock's sandwiches, aware she wasn't doing justice to the preparations but simply too tired to be really hungry. And when the older woman finally paused to draw breath, Alix finally managed to express gratitude for all her work.

'I really can't thank you enough,' she said honestly. The house revealed careful attention, and obviously Mrs Babcock had spent a great deal of time cleaning and dusting and making it pleasant for Alix's arrival.

'Nothing to it,' came the reply. 'I always think first impressions are important, and there could be nothing worse than to end a marathon drive like you've had to be faced with a cleaning job, or nothing fresh to eat, or . . .'

'Or not being able to sleep through worry, which is one problem you've certainly saved me, Mrs Babcock,' Alix interrupted gently. 'In fact I'm going to have trouble not falling asleep right here in this chair . . .'

'Well, you certainly can't do that,' was the reply. 'Now off with you to bed and I'll just take a minute to do these dishes so you don't have to face them in the morning. You'll be wanting the dog in with you, I'm sure, and don't worry, I'll put him in as I leave. Now off with you—and no arguments!'

The stern command came with a broad, motherly smile, and Alix decided it would be easier to obey than to argue her own responsibilities about dishes and things. Struggling out of her chair, she beat a hasty retreat to the bedroom and started looking for the nightgown she had packed.

She was in the small, well-appointed bathroom, staring at the shower and debating if she had the energy to use it, when Mrs Babcock trilled, 'I'm going now, dear. Key's on the table and here's your fine big dog.' Then a liver-coloured nose thrust open the door and nudged itself into Alix's palm as Nick began to wuffle-wuffle-wuffle for attention.

'Get out of here, you great sook,' Alix snorted at him, 'Can't a girl even take a shower in private?'

Rejected, he turned away to sprawl out beside the bed, and Alix summoned the energy to get into the shower and at least get clean before she slept. And once beneath the steaming caress of the shower, she felt her healthy young body sloughing off its fatigue with the travel dust; humming softly to herself as she forced shampoo through her long hair, she felt fresher than she had at any time since leaving Melbourne.

It was an absolutely super little cottage, she thought, roaming casually through the tidy rooms in her housecoat as she ran a brush through her hair. Of course it couldn't compare with her parents' house, which she had left in the hands of a rental agent, but for her present needs, it was ideal. No room for entertaining, of course, but then she would hardly be doing much of that, at least not for the moment.

How could she ... not knowing anyone? The only person she had met thus far, apart from dear Mrs Babcock, was hardly the type she would be thinking of entertaining here at home. Arrogant fellow! But handsome, in a rough-hewn sort of fashion, she couldn't deny that.

Perhaps it was just as well that she wouldn't be likely to meet him again. He was just a bit too ... masculine ... and certainly he wouldn't be as easily controllable as Bruce. But then what had controlling Bruce ever got her? Alix shuddered at memories best forgotten, and as the gentle monotony of brushing her hair eased back her tiredness, she retired to her new bedroom and lay back in the darkness.

Her small travel alarm clock seemed to be lying to her; it couldn't possibly be only eight-thirty, she thought. So she checked her watch against the alarm, found that both of them agreed, and a moment later she was drifting towards sleep. Her final conscious thoughts were not, for once, of Bruce and his deceit, but of a nameless man with green-fire eyes and coffee-coloured hair.

Almost ten hours later she was nudged into wakefulness by Nick, who demanded to be allowed outside to greet the rising sun, and Alix threw on her housecoat and joined him, revelling in the feel of the chilly dew upon her bare feet as she stepped out into the enormous yard for her first daylight look at the place.

It quickly became obvious that Nick had done his share of exploring the night before. He paid a brief visit to the bottom of the garden, then danced back to tug at Alix's hem, pulling her gently towards the corner of the big house and the kennels that had been constructed there.

Curious at his insistence, she ignored the chill of the damp ground and followed him, almost shrieking with delighted surprise as she saw the lone occupant of the four-kennel complex.

'Oh, you little beauty!' she exclaimed, kneeling to reach through the wire as the excited G.S.P. bitch danced to the front of the run and sat trembling with excitement as she crooned her wuffle-wuffle-wuffle of greeting. Slightly smaller than Nick, but obviously in prime condition, the bitch was solid liver in colour except for a tiny splash of ticking on her forehead, and her coat gleamed with obvious conditioning. Her half-docked tail quivered, in constant motion, as her eyes flickered from Alix to Nick and back again.

Alix spent several minutes squatting at the door of the run, talking softly to the liver bitch, but when Nick began to loudly whinge his desire to get closer to the other dog, Alix decided it was time to go. She wasn't about to start off her residency here with bad feelings by disturbing somebody else's dog, and by the look of the bitch she was a valued possession whose owner might take a dim view of Alix disrupting the bitch's routine.

'Besides, you'll have to be thinking of other things, at least today,' she told her disappointed companion. 'Now come and have breakfast and start thinking about work for a change.'

The dog wolfed down his own meal as Alix prepared a quick breakfast of toast and eggs and tea, then he sat obediently by the door as she collected everything they would need.

Nick's water bowl, a flask of fresh, cool water, his collar and lead, registration papers, her own documentation as his handler, immunisation certificates, and finally the map Mr Jennings had sent her showing how to reach the grounds where today's trials were being held by the Bundaberg Obedience Dog Club.

It had been exceptionally kind of Mr Jennings, Alix thought. Not only had he arranged this super little cottage for her, but, knowing her interest in dog obedience work, he had also sent her a copy of the local club's monthly newsletter in time for her to enter the trial.

She double-checked her list, then hurriedly slipped into a new forest-green track suit and gathered her long hair into a flowing chestnut ponytail.

'Right . . . we're off,' she said gaily, and the big dog leaped erect to wait trembling at the door. He needed no urging to get him into the station wagon; Nick knew perfectly well that track suits and training gear meant a pleasurable day's outing.

Alix knew she was leaving far too early, since the trial wasn't scheduled to begin until ten, which meant she should arrive by nine-thirty. She wanted the extra time to give Nick a really good run, in hopes that he'd wear off some of the excess energy he had collected during the long, two-day drive from Melbourne.

And besides, it was such a truly beautiful morning. No matter that to native Queenslanders it was the middle of winter; for Alix it was like a return to springtime after the blustery, rainy weather of Melbourne.

She found her way downtown without difficulty, marvelling at the scarcity of traffic, and decided there would be time to check out Mr Jennings' third map and find the place she would be going to work. Five minutes later she was in the Bunda Industrial Estate at the western edge of the city, looking at the tidy engineering complex where she would be reporting for duty next morning.

Very nice, she thought. Serviceable, but neatly constructed and, at least from the outside, it looked like the type of place where the workers took a certain amount of pride in their surroundings and their work.

'Tomorrow will tell the tale, anyway,' she muttered aloud, turning to retrace her route into the city area and across the high Burnett River traffic bridge to North Bundaberg. Mr Jennings drew a good map; she found herself at the Musgrave Pony Club grounds and the obedience dog club just before nine o'clock.

'Okay, dog . . . time for a thorough workout,' she told the grinning G.S.P. Nick required no further coaxing; he bounced out of the station wagon and began an immediate, pacing inspection of the trial grounds and the open scrub country around them.

The next person to arrive was the lady president of the Bundaberg club, and the honorary veterinarian was right behind her. Alix introduced herself, arranged the final competition details, and had Nick vetted before any of the other dogs had even arrived.

Organised at last, she took Nick into the paddock behind the trial grounds and began a serious training session.

His earlier run had burned off sufficient energy to make him reasonably biddable, but Alix found he was still a bit too easily distracted for her liking. He did his heeling exercises and retrieving excellently, and she expected no problems there, but as usual he turned a deaf ear to her commmands to drop on recall.

He *could* do it. Indeed, he had done it perfectly during the last two trials where he had gained qualification in the open division. Only one more qualification and he could add the 'CDX' Companion Dog Excellence title to his list of show and obedience awards. But somehow Alix sensed that today he was going to be difficult, and she resolved to put him through the exercise over and over until, with luck, he would do it by rote when the proper moment arrived.

Ignoring the babble of new arrivals and the jeers and instructions between workers setting up the trial rings, she worked Nick back and forth, using both hand signals and voice commands. 'Come . . . drop!' Again and again and again.

'I'd give it a rest, if I were you. You'll have him bored with the whole thing by the time he competes.'

The voice from behind her startled Alix so badly she spun too quickly on the dewy grass and slipped quite off balance. But strong hands caught her even as her own, involuntarily, grasped at the Harris tweed jacket before her. Then she looked up to meet startling green eyes, eyes like green fire, or green ice . . . and she recoiled abruptly.

'Don't panic,' he said with a wicked little grin. 'I'm not planning to collect my rain check yet. It's a bit . . . public?'

'I should certainly hope so,' Alix retorted, inwardly wishing Nick would charge over and bite this intrusive stranger on the leg. Not that he would, of course. Oh no. Instead the traitorous animal trotted over to sit politely and wait to be noticed.

'Well, you're none the worse for your experience, I see,' the man said softly, kneeling to run his knuckles over Nick's head and then scratch him softly behind the ears. He was rewarded with a friendly wuffle-wuffle-wuffle, and Alix could have kicked him.

'Nick . . . heel!' she ordered grimly, and gained a measure of satisfaction when the dog quickly picked himself up and trotted round to sit by her left leg.

'Pity they docked his tail so short; he isn't a bad-looking specimen otherwise,' the tall man observed casually, and Alix immediately bristled in the dog's defence despite her knowledge that the comment was a fair one.

'It's just right,' she countered hotly. 'Certainly it hasn't stopped him from winning most of his classes so far. He's already qualified as an Australian Champion.'

'Don't get all huffy; it was only a personal opinion,' he replied calmly. 'How's he doing in obedience work?'

'He's one qualification short for his CDX title, and he should have that today,' she replied proudly, and just a little saucily.

'You sound pretty confident,' he said, raising one dark eyebrow suspiciously. 'Got the judge in your pocket or something?'

'I *resent* that!'

'Oh? You wore that rather sexy track suit to impress the other dogs, did you?'

'Don't be ridiculous. It isn't at all sexy,' Alix replied, seeing her own lie reflected by the gleam of appreciation in his eyes. The soft cloth of the outfit moulded her slender body quite attractively and she knew it, but impressing an obedience trials judge was the last thing she would have considered. 'I only wore it because it's warm,' she concluded, flushing slightly at the quirky little grin he threw her.

'Just as well, because I happen to know that the open division judge today wouldn't be swayed even by you,' he said. 'Just as well you aren't in Novice, though. That judge is a woman, and she might take exception to being shown up by a competitor.'

'Really? And tell me, who are *you* trying to show up?' Alix responded rather tartly. Certainly his expensive tweed jacket, combined with equally expensive slacks and leisure boots and even a necktie, seemed rather out of place in this setting.

Most of the men were in jeans and T-shirts or shorts and running shoes, with the female competitors similarly attired. A substantial number of Bundaberg Obedience Dog Club T-shirts revealed a good working group of stewards and officials.

'I have no need to show anyone up,' the tall man replied icily. 'Especially since I'm not competing.'

'What a pity,' Alix sneered. 'I'm sure the lady judge in Novice class would have been suitably impressed. Now if you don't mind, I'd like to run Nick through that exercise a few times yet.'

'Be my guest,' he replied lightly. 'But if he comes into the trial bored out of his mind, don't say I didn't warn you. And while you're at it, you might try leaning forward a bit when you give him the 'drop' signal. Waving your arm as high as you are seems to be part of his problem.'

'Thank you very much, but I hardly think I need any advice from you,' she replied carelessly. 'We've been doing just fine so far without it.'

'Your privilege,' he replied, turning away. 'And good luck.'

'Thank you,' Alix replied, suddenly a little ashamed at having been so brusque. But he *did* manage to raise her hackles, this fellow. Just her luck to have him show up here, of all places! What bothered her even more was that he might be right, but when she glanced across the field he was standing, watching her, so she defiantly ignored all his advice and tried to forget it as the loudhailer called all competitors to get ready.

She arrived just in time for the introduction of the day's judges, and her astonishment at seeing *that* man introduced as one of them faded quickly to despair with the realisation that he would be judging the open class. Quinn Tennant, his name was; that much Alix was certain of. But did she only imagine the saucy wink he casually dropped when he caught her staring at him, her cheeks flushed with embarrassment?

'How do I get myself into these things?' she moaned half aloud, oblivious to the curious stares her comment drew from several other competitors. Alix was fifth in a class of twelve, and by the time the first three were finished, her worst fears had been realised. This man was a tough judge.

She saw a splendid German Shepherd zeroed for sitting just a little bit crooked after returning from his retrieve, and a Dobermann who gave the judge a dirty look during the 'Stand for Examination' paid for it in points. How would he regard Nick's invariably over-friendly reaction to the examination? she wondered.

She hardly noticed the fourth competitor's performance, too busy building up problems in her mind, and when her number was finally called, she moved towards the ring with less confidence than she had ever felt before.

The green track suit, so comfortable only moments before, suddenly seemed to turn into an oven, and she was conscious of its clinging to her every curve. Not that this Tennant man seemed to mind; he was regarding her with a smile that seemed to Alix to portray an advanced case of lechery, and the knowledge that it was all in her own mind didn't help a bit.

During the fast-pace heeling exercise, her lack of a bra suddenly seemed the height of folly, and her concentration wavered between keeping an even pace for Nick and trying to slow the movement of her breasts. Quinn Tennant merely grinned encouragingly, or so it must have looked to the spectators. Alix knew he was enjoying her discomfiture almost as much as the movement of her body.

Her nervousness was communicating itself to Nick, which was perhaps the worst part of it all. Alix kept having to stop herself from looking down to see if he was even still with her, and if she had suddenly found him sitting by the judge's side, it would have been no surprise at all.

Quinn Tennant gave her his instructions in exactly the same tone of voice he had used for those before her, but in Alix's ears the voice insinuated things that certainly didn't belong in any obedience trial. Oh, damn you, she thought. It's all deliberate on your part. You know very well you're getting to me, and you're enjoying every bit of it.

She was so busy hating him she almost missed his instruction about the drop on recall, and he was forced to ask twice if she was ready. 'Y—y—yes,' she finally stammered, fuming inwardly at the complacent, smug grin he gave her.

She knew before she had even left Nick that it wasn't going to come off. He was sitting properly, but the big dog's eyes were flicking from side to side as he waited for the command, and Alix cringed inside.

'Call him,' came the instruction, very quietly spoken.

Alix waved her arm. 'Come!'

'Drop him.'

She threw every ounce of willpower into the command, even stooping slightly as she had been advised. 'Drop!' she screamed, loud enough to be heard in Melbourne.

And miracle of miracles, Nick dropped like a stone, only his stub of a tail flickering his impatience with the command Alix knew he considered illogical.

'Call him.'

She did, and the great dog thundered forward with such velocity Alix half expected to be knocked off her feet.

'Exercise complete,' Quinn Tennant said in his judging voice, and then, under his breath as Alix passed him, 'Glad to see you take advice *sometimes*.'

She went rigid, knowing she didn't dare to reply. And through the remainder of the exercises she held herself under strict control, not meeting his eyes for fear she would say something regrettable. Nick bounced through the retrieves without a hitch, cleared the broad jump easily and correctly, and finished the first part of the programme with the highest score thus far. If he could just hang on through the 'stays', he would have his third qualification without any problems, and Alix spent the time the rest of her class was being tested walking the big dog back and forth to settle him down.

They went in as a class for the 'sit-stay', and when the handlers had left their dogs and gathered out of their sight behind the canteen, the owner of the highest-scoring German Shepherd complimented Alix on her dog and her luck with Quinn Tennant.

'I don't understand,' she replied. And then, 'Oh! He doesn't fancy G.S.P.s, you mean?'

'No such thing,' the young man replied. 'They're about the only breed he does like, which makes him tougher on them because he expects them to be superior. If you get through this your dog'll be the first G.S.P. I've ever seen Tennant qualify.'

'Oh,' replied Alix, wondering if the sudden unease that shot through her like an electric current was revealed in her face. 'Well, maybe I'll be lucky. Nick usually never falters in the stays.'

And when they returned, finally, at the steward's direction, she was uncommonly relieved to find Nick sitting, just as ordered, and showing no sign of movement. Alix praised him mightily after the exercise had been declared complete, but half her mind was on the tall man whose green eyes had drunk in her every movement as they had walked back into the ring.

More and more, she regretted having worn the clinging track suit, because after they had dropped the dogs and again left the ring, this time for a full five minutes, she could feel Quinn Tennant's eyes following her, undressing her both in his mind and her own.

When the young man with the German Shepherd offered Alix a cigarette as they waited through the five minutes that dragged like five hours, she took it, fumbled it nervously and dropped it in the sand.

'Hang on; steady up,' he said kindly. 'I'm sorry if I upset you with what I said.'

'It isn't that,' she replied, no longer trying to hide her nervousness. But she didn't continue; how could she possibly reveal to this stranger the unsettling effect that another stranger was having on her?

She almost jumped out of her skin when she heard the out-of-sight commotion that confirmed at least one of the dogs had broken his long drop, and something inside her screamed at the knowledge that it had been Nick. Of course the handlers weren't allowed to know which dog it was, not until they returned to the ring and could see for themselves.

Alix shuddered, remembering a trial in Melbourne when one dog had unaccountably lifted from his stay and walked the entire line of competitors, each of them rising to follow him until the entire class had been disqualified. Usually, a steward would attempt to prevent such an occurrence, but on that fateful occasion the judge had forbidden it, saying it was no more than another element to the test itself.

Finally they were called back to the ring, and Alix's heart-stopping relief that it hadn't been Nick who had broken was immediately displaced by the realisation that Quinn Tennant was once again watching her. The bright green eyes were alive with a deliberate masculine assessment, one that became even more disconcerting as Alix was forced to swivel her hips through the homemade turnstile into the trial grounds.

She moved with one eye on Nick and the other on Quinn Tennant, whose smile seemed to be aimed at her alone. The grin widened as she stumbled, throwing out one arm to regain her balance as she lurched forward until she could almost touch the ground with her fingers.

'Oh!' The cry was involuntary, but the 'damn!' that followed was quite deliberate.

Alix didn't need to hear Nick's low growl of instinctive protection; she saw from the corner of her eye the deliberate tensing of his muscles as he eased himself half upright, then slowly subsided into the drop position again as Alix regained her own balance and her place in line.

Disqualified! There was no room for doubt, because even as she glanced up to see if Quinn Tennant had noticed, the cocked eyebrow revealed that he had. The rest was a foregone conclusion, although of course Alix went through the formality of finishing off the exercise, glaring defiantly at Quinn Tennant as she did so despite the sinking feeling of despair that filled her stomach.

She wasn't surprised to see the zero go up on the score board after her number, but Quinn Tennant's 'Hard luck,' after they had left the ring was sufficiently unsympathetic to gain him a snarled reply.

'It wasn't Nick's fault,' she declared angrily. Damn, damn, damn! Nick had done everything else properly, had even ignored the distraction of another dog breaking his stay—a move which had drawn six of the twelve competitors into disqualification. For him to be disqualified for a perfectly understandable reaction was just ... just unfair.

Alix could have cared less about not qualifying. Much as she enjoyed obedience work, it was the pleasure of working with her dog that provided the real pleasure, not the titles and trophies. Still, it was damnably unfair. And doubly so because of Quinn Tennant's attitude.

'My dear girl,' he said in a tone that could only be described as totally condescending, 'it is *never* the dog's fault. Surely even you must realise there are no bad dogs, only bad handlers.'

'Well, I wouldn't have tripped if you hadn't ...' Alix stopped, unable to bring forth her accusation. What would it sound like, discounting the obvious counter-charge of vanity, conceit and a deliberate attempt to sway the judge?

'If I hadn't? If I hadn't what?' Quinn Tennant's voice held a tone of amused scorn that only served to make Alix even more angry, but not quite enough to make her answer. So he did it for her.

'I suppose you were going to say if I hadn't been watching you. And why shouldn't I? Or do you intend to maintain your fictitious claim that you wore that outfit only to keep warm?'

'That's despicable! I always wear a track suit to compete, at least in winter. And besides, there are several other girls wearing them today, and I don't hear anybody complaining.'

'You don't hear me complaining either,' he replied with a malicious grin. 'I think it's rather fetching; I just hope it doesn't shrink the first time you wash it.'

'What . . . what are you talking about?' Alix stammered. But she knew, even before he reached out to take her by the shoulders and turn her around. She felt his fingers brushing past her bottom and then his hand reached over her shoulder to wave the evidence in front of her horrified eyes.

'And worth every penny,' he said very softly, dangling the price tag until Alix reached up angrily to snatch it from his fingers.

Her face burned. She had to force herself to turn and meet his eyes once again. Her mind raced like an engine out of gear; she was mortifyingly embarrassed at the thought of having paraded through the entire morning in a track suit with the price tag hanging from the back. And he had known it all along, she suddenly realised. He would have seen it when he came up behind her out on the field, long before hardly anyone had shown up, at a time when he could have told her.

Quinn Tennant didn't bother to hedge around it. 'Yes, I knew,' he admitted with a blatant lack of concern.

'Well, you might have told me!'

'Why? None of my business. And I've already had a substantial share of your reaction to advice,' he replied. 'And besides, how was I supposed to know it wasn't deliberate?'

He caught her swinging hand only inches from his face, gripping her wrist in a clamp of iron fingers that didn't hurt her, but kept her so totally immobile that he could stare down into her angry eyes and half-open, gasping lips. And Nick, who had been so eager to defend her earlier that he had disqualified himself, now sat traitorously at ease beside her, tail twitching happily as if he, too, was enjoying the spectacle.

'And don't curse, either,' Quinn Tennant cautioned her. 'I don't like girls who swear.'

'You . . . let . . . me . . . go . . . or I'll scream the place down around your ears!' Alix hissed through tight-clenched teeth. 'I'm sure it would do your reputation the world of good to be seen abusing a woman . . .'

'Stop being bloody ridiculous,' he snapped, cutting off her threat in mid-sentence. 'Who's going to pay the slightest bit of attention to a disgruntled competitor arguing with the judge? Now if I were to do a little debt collecting . . .'

Again, that horribly mocking grin. And as he moved his head infinitesimally toward her, Alix recoiled as if he were going to hit her.

'You . . . you . . . bastard!' she hissed.

'I'm not, you know,' he replied with a broad grin, then released her hand and stepped quickly back out of range. Then his eyes took on a distinctly kindly expression and he asked softly, 'Is winning really all that important to you?'

How to answer? For some reason Alix felt a deep inner longing to simply admit the truth. It didn't matter a whit, although she was honestly sorry that the disqualification, while legitimate, was solely her own fault. But to admit that to this arrogant, mocking man . . .?

'I . . . I just don't like to see Nick suffer for something that wasn't his fault,' she replied somewhat lamely. And he laughed.

'*Nick* suffer? Oh, come now. He isn't going to suffer at all. Unless of course you're the type that goes off and beats their dog for human mistakes.'

His lips twisted in a wry grin. 'No, Nick isn't going to suffer. Why should he? He only did what he thought was right. The only suffering there'll be is to your own pride, my girl, because the mistake was yours. And you know it and I know it and everybody else knows it. So why not forget it? If you *must* get all flustered about the whole thing, just try and remember next time to watch where you're going. If you'd paid more attention to that and less to me, you wouldn't have the problem in the first place.'

'You're obviously convinced that I only stumbled because I was watching you,' Alix replied scathingly. 'Personally, I think that's horribly conceited and arrogant of you.'

'Probably. But it isn't important,' he replied with great aplomb. 'Now come and I'll buy you a coffee before they start the U.D. trials, which I very much want to see.'

'I'll buy my own coffee,' she snarled, but he already had reached out to take her by the arm and escort her toward the canteen, and despite Alix's unobtrusive attempts to free herself, he kept his grip and moved her along with him as if she belonged there, not releasing her until they had joined the crush at the canteen.

There, he held her with his eyes as he ordered their coffee, paid for it, and handed her cup over with a friendly, normal smile. Alix dearly wanted to throw it in his face, but she could hardly do so in this crowd. When he gestured towards the ring where the U.D.—Utility Dog—trials were about to start, she moved along with him despite her inner seething.

CHAPTER THREE

'QUINN ... darling!' Both Quinn Tennant and Alix turned at the voice, she in curiosity and the man himself with obvious pleasure.

The woman who strode up and threw her arms around Quinn Tennant's neck was about Alix's height, but perhaps a bit more slender. She had quite long, wavy dark brown hair and eyes of the same colour that fairly sparkled with pleasure. Her beauty was not classic, but she had excellent bones, a broad, rather sensuous mouth and small even teeth.

It was the sensuous mouth that reached up to meet Quinn Tennant's as his arms slid around the woman's waist to lift her close against him.

'Michelle! I thought you were in Brisbane this weekend,' he replied, but not until they had kissed for what seemed to Alix an inappropriately lengthy interval.

'Obviously,' the woman replied with an arch of her tidy eyebrows. 'Aren't you going to introduce me to your ... friend?'

Ha! Let's see him get out of this one, Alix thought. But even as she did so, he had turned to introduce the two women.

'Michelle Keir ... Alix McLean,' he said, and as Alix stood there, her mouth half open in astonishment, he continued, 'Alix is up from Melbourne, and you'll have to excuse her expression. She's just had a bit of bad luck with old Nick, here, in the open class.'

Alix was stunned. How could he possibly know her name, and that she was from Melbourne? Pondering this, she could only nod in reply to the other woman's greeting as Quinn Tennant went on to explain about Alix having stumbled and Nick responding so disastrously.

'And you, of course, couldn't make the slightest allow-

44

ance,' Michelle Keir chuckled, showing her teeth in a patronising grin. 'Especially not with one of your precious G.S.P.s involved.'

He shrugged. 'Nothing to do with the breed of dog. He broke his stay and that's all there was to it.' To Alix's vague surprise, he continued to describe the problem with no reference at all to either their confrontation or her own ineptness.

How did he know her name? She thought back, then almost sighed with relief. He must have got it from the entry forms . . . but when? Being a local judge, he couldn't help but know some of the competitors, but it wouldn't be considered ethical for a judge to see the entry list before an event. He should have been operating solely from the entry numbers. It was all too confusing, and Alix found her mind so occupied trying to figure it out that Quinn Tennant had to speak twice to get her attention.

'I'm . . . sorry,' she stammered. 'I was . . . thinking of something.'

'You shouldn't try to think and walk at the same time,' he grinned mischievously. 'You might stumble again.' Then, ignoring her flush of indignation, 'I asked how old Nick is.'

'He was three last month,' Alix replied absently, her mind still whirling madly.

'He's a very nice-looking dog, for a G.S.P.,' Michelle Keir murmured politely, and the remark drew a harsh bark of laughter from Quinn Tennant.

'Don't be catty, Michelle,' he replied rather sternly, and then spoke to Alix in a tone that seemed rather conde- scending to the dark-haired woman. 'Michelle thinks Sam- oyeds are the only dogs in the world,' he said. 'Personally I couldn't imagine a less suitable animal, especially here in Queensland, but some women have no taste.'

Somewhat to Alix's surprise, the other woman laughed gaily at the quip without apparent offence. 'At least my dogs have some personality,' she responded. 'Look at that beast there—he couldn't care less about people. No of- fence, Alix, of course.'

'That's only because he knows damned well he's a dog

and is proud of it,' Quinn Tennant replied before Alix
could say a word. 'Those Sams of yours are all right in their
place, which I might point out is in the Arctic, not subtropical Queensland, but everywhere else they're nothing
but lapdogs. And yours are even worse, because *they* think
they *are* people.'

'But they are, darling. And no matter how much you
stand up for your so-called working gun-dogs, you know
very well my Samoyeds are smarter—and nicer—than
most people, at least most people I know.'

'Including me,' he laughed. 'Not least because I won't
let your eighty-pound horrors up on my lap.'

'True, but I'll continue to make allowances for you as
long as you don't object to *me* sitting on your lap,' replied
Michelle, and Alix got the distinct impression the comment was aimed more at herself than at Quinn Tennant,
who merely grunted an unreadable response.

'And anyway, Alix doesn't want to hear about our
doggie disagreements,' Michelle continued. 'Especially not
as she seems just as converted as you are. Tell me, Alix,
what brings you to Bundaberg?'

'She's a design draughtsman, or draughtswoman, if you
prefer,' Quinn Tennant replied, and Alix sat dumbfounded as he went on to explain, telling Michelle the
company Alix would be working for.

How could he know? It simply wasn't possible, Alix
thought, but she had no opportunity to ask because the
first entrant in the U.D. competition was entering the ring
and Quinn Tennant immediately shushed both women to
silence.

Michelle Keir sat obediently quiet, one arm tucked
through Quinn's and her long, slender fingers stroking his
thigh as she ostensibly watched the judging. Despite her
internal confusion, Alix found the gesture quite out of
place, but she found her eyes constantly drawn to the
hypnotic movement of the long-nailed, manicured fingers.

Certainly this woman considered she had some kind of
claim on Quinn Tennant, Alix thought. And welcome to
him, at that. Arrogant devil. Not that it explained her own
reaction to the warm pressure of his thigh against hers, not

to mention the arm so carelessly flung along the bench top behind her.

How could this man possibly know about her? And worse . . . how much did he know? Her mind awhirl with speculation and wonder, she didn't realise for a moment that he had somehow slipped his arm lower, his fingers brushing casually against her shoulder.

Strange tingles ran through Alix at the touch of those fingers, and she had to restrain the urge to snuggle back against his hand like a cat wanting to be petted. Then her eyes slid down to where Michelle's lacquered nails still caressed Quinn's thigh, and she flinched away as if his fingers burned her.

The nerve of him! Alix shook her head in disbelief at the audacity of a man who could caress one woman while being caressed himself by another. Her anger surged up as her movement broke the physical contact between them, but Quinn seemed not to notice. It wasn't until Alix spoke, excusing herself, that he turned to look at her.

'You're leaving so soon?' Nothing in the words, or those bright green eyes, to reveal his understanding of her intentions. Surely he must have been aware that he was touching her, Alix thought, surprised to find herself equally angry at the thought that he might not have been.

'I really have a great deal to do at home,' she replied steadily, fighting the urge to avoid his bland eyes. 'I just moved in yesterday, you see, and I still haven't even unpacked.'

'Don't badger the girl, Quinn,' Michelle interrupted, her fingers tightening ever so slightly on his thigh. 'Just because you can live half your life out of a suitcase it doesn't mean she has to.'

It was clear enough to Alix that she represented an unwanted third, and for a second she entertained the quixotic thought of staying on just to spite Michelle Keir. But why, for goodness' sake? She herself had no interest in Quinn Tennant, and just because the dark-haired woman for some reason set her teeth on edge . . .

'And she does, too,' Alix told a totally uninterested Nick as they drove homeward. She knew very well that the woman's stylish appearance, especially when contrasted to her own outfit, certainly had something to do with it, but there was something else involved as well. The woman had a . . . something . . . a sort of catty, or better yet, vixenish aura about her. Yes, foxy . . . especially around the eyes and those tiny, ever-so-white teeth.

It was mildly disturbing, because Alix seldom found herself with an instinctive dislike for other women. It would be different, of course, if she fancied Quinn Tennant herself, but despite his unarguable handsomeness, he held no real attraction. And just because he had kissed her once there was no reason to think she held any attraction for him . . . him and his presumptuous rain check!

Nick sprawled out for a nap when they got home, leaving Alix alone to finish unpacking and fix herself a light lunch. But just as she felt like napping, he insisted on being let out.

'All right, but *no* barking, and *no* digging, and *no* disturbing that pretty little bitch in the kennels,' she said, smiling to herself as the big dog danced his way across the lawn in a beeline for the third 'no'. He'd be back in a minute, she thought, sprawling out on the sofa to await his habitual wuffle at the door.

But it wasn't Nick's wuffle that woke her nearly two hours later. It was a bellowing voice, somehow rather familiar, shouting, 'Nick! Get the hell out of it! Anna . . . heel!'

Startled into a confused wakefulness, Alix threw open the door and dashed out into the yard to find Nick and the liver-coloured bitch chasing madly about, leaping and twisting in frenzied excitement and then trotting side by side with their peculiar, walking-on-eggs gait as they patrolled the boundaries.

And standing at one corner of the house, Michelle Keir directly behind him with a secretive smirk on her face as he swore at the dashing dogs, was Quinn Tennant.

'Who the hell told you you could let her out of that kennel?' he demanded as Alix stepped through the doorway, and as she stood there, totally confused, he shouted even louder, 'Dammit—answer me! You should know better than that.'

'But I ...' She couldn't go on. He was ignoring her, reaching out to grab his bitch as she pranced up to sit facing him, tongue lolling out in welcome. Then Nick, too, wheeled into line and sat, one paw uplifted in the shake-hands gesture Alix often found so amusing.

'Come on, Anna, back in your run,' Quinn Tennant muttered gently, leading the bitch with a firm yet tender grip on the scruff of her neck. Suddenly compliant, she followed beside him, trying meanwhile to look back at her new-found playmate.

Nick whined, obviously not amused at having their game so quickly disrupted, and Quinn turned to speak quietly to him. 'It's all right, old man. You'll just have to wait until you get permission for this kind of thing. *My* permission,' he added very distinctly with a direct glare at Alix.

His permission? *Anna's going to love him* ... the words echoed in Alix's mind as memory mingled with surprise.

'Anna,' she said thoughtfully. 'She's *your* dog, then, so this is ...'

'My house,' he concluded for her.

'Then Mrs ... Babcock is ... your ...'

'Housekeeper will do.'

'And of course you're my landlord.' It all fell into place now. This was how he had known her name, her business, everything. Even now, those bright green eyes were laughing at her.

'I suppose you even knew who I was when we met on the road last night.' It wasn't exactly a question, but the look on Michelle Keir's face indicated that an answer would be forthcoming, later if not right now.

Quinn Tennant laughed. 'It wasn't exactly hard to guess, let's put it that way.'

Alix didn't quite trust herself to reply to such a blatant attitude. To give herself time to think, she called Nick to her and reached down to take a grip on the scruff of his neck. The big dog accepted this briefly, then twisted away from her and trotted to sit quietly at heel.

Alix looked up to meet Quinn Tennant's unreadable

eyes. 'I get the impression you think it's all very funny,' she said then. She was beginning to seethe inside, her stomach roiled and boiling with growing anger.

He shrugged. Not important, the gesture said.

'Well, I don't,' Alix replied to the unspoken avoidance of a reply. 'In fact I think it's rather childish.'

Michelle giggled slightly at that, but Quinn Tennant said nothing for a moment. When he did speak, there was no humour in his eyes.

'Is that why you let my dog out?'

'I did not—repeat, not—let your dog out,' Alix retorted, then shrunk back at his scathing gesture of disbelief.

'I suppose *he* did,' Quinn Tennant replied in obvious contempt. 'Or are you going to try and make me believe that he and Anna managed it between them?'

At the sound of her name, the liver bitch whined a reply, and Nick responded by trotting over to rear high on his hind legs and nudge at the gate with his long Roman nose.

'I haven't the faintest idea how your dog got out,' Alix said angrily. 'All I know is that I had nothing to do with it.'

'Frankly, Miss McLean, I think you're having me on,' Quinn Tennant replied grimly. His eyes revealed an obvious contempt for what even Alix admitted must sound like a ridiculous lie, but she was too angry to care. She hadn't let the dog out, and she knew it no matter what anyone else might think.

'Frankly, Mr Tennant, I couldn't care less what you believe,' she retorted scathingly. 'Nick, get out of that!'

Nick responded immediately, but as he turned away from the gate it swung open behind him and Anna followed right on his stubby little tail.

Alix and Quinn Tennant stood in stunned silence, but Michelle burst out in a peal of tinkling laughter as the two dogs grinned their pleasure and trotted away to the bottom of the garden.

'I think,' Michelle said finally, 'that you owe Miss McLean an apology, Quinn dear.'

He said nothing. Alix said nothing either, for a moment. Instead she walked over and looked suspiciously at the gate latch, reaching over to close it and open it several times. Then, using the heel of her hand, she pushed against the gate and latch and stifled an exclamation as it sprang open immediately.

So Nick *had* opened the gate the first time! There was no question about the exhibition they had just witnessed, but Alix's own fingers had just proved it was no fluke. She turned to Quinn Tennant, making no effort to hide her feelings.

They stood glaring at one another for several seconds before Alix trusted herself to speak.

'Well?' she said.

'Well what?'

'Well, it appears that my dog is considerably more intelligent than you give him credit for,' she replied. 'And I *also* think you owe me an apology.'

Quinn Tennant grinned, but there was little humour in it. Then he shrugged. 'I certainly owe Nick an apology,' he admitted, 'but I fail to see why you deserve one.'

Alix's mouth dropped open in astonishment. How could he say such a thing? He had accused her unjustly, and seen for himself the proof that his accusation was unjust. And now, to blithely deny that he owed her any apology . . .

'Don't be stupid!' she snapped.

His eyebrows raised in silent query. 'Stupid?'

'You heard me.'

'Of course I heard you. I may be . . . stupid . . . but I'm not deaf,' he retorted, jaw muscles quivering with ill-disguised anger. 'Now I'd like an explanation of your choice of words.'

'It's perfectly obvious,' Alix snapped. Then, deliberately, she slowed her words into a litany as if explaining something complex to a backward child.

'You accused me of opening that gate. I did not. You accused me of lying. I did not. You accused me trying to to fool you by saying my dog opened the gate. I did not. The fact that he did open the gate is obvious. Therefore you owe me an apology.'

During her recital, Quinn Tennant seemed to have regained at least some of his composure. His words, when they finally emerged, held a calm self-assurance that was almost as frightening as his anger.

'Your dog has shown rather surprising intelligence—agreed,' he began. 'I therefore apologise to him for not believing him capable of opening the gate. To you, however, I make no apology whatsoever, Miss McLean, since I consider *you* to be responsible for your dog's actions. In future, I would suggest that you maintain better control of him. Is that perfectly clear?'

Alix was speechless. Clear? It certainly was! Her mouth, hanging open with surprise, snapped shut as blinding rage took over her consciousness. The arrogance . . . the unspeakable arrogance of this man . . . brought forth emotions she hadn't ever believed existed inside her. Even the deliberate and callous treatment she had received from Bruce hadn't created such a vivid desire for physical revenge. Her fingers clawed by her sides as she stood in rigid silence, destroying Quinn Tennant with her eyes, slicing him to ribbons, tearing out his black heart and throwing it upon the ground.

'It . . . is . . . perfectly clear,' she ground out, then turned on her heel and strode back to her open doorway, flinging a demanding call to Nick as she turned. The big dog, surprisingly, trotted obediently over to follow her inside, starting violently with the realisation that if he had had a full-length tail it would have been cropped by the slamming door behind him.

'O . . . o . . . o . . . oooooooh!' she screamed to herself after Quinn Tennant had shut away his dog and walked from sight around the corner of the house with Michelle Keir clinging to his arm.

'Oh, you arrogant, chauvinistic, rotten *swine*! Inconsiderate . . . narrow-minded . . . egotistical . . .' She couldn't go on. Tears suddenly rushed into her eyes and she flung herself on to the bed in a paroxysm of uncontrollable weeping that went on and on and on.

Eventually she cried the frustration out of her system, but even the tears couldn't remove the hot anger at the unfairness of it all. The incident with Quinn Tennant had stolen, for ever—it seemed—the pleasure of her fine new home.

'Well, you can keep it and be damned to you,' Alix suddenly cried aloud. Striding angrily into the bathroom, she splashed cold water onto her red, tear-swollen eyes, then returned to begin all over the packing of everything she had unpacked only hours before.

She flung dresses and slacks indiscriminately into her suitcases, tore the few cherished books from their new home on the cottage's spacious bookshelves, and snarled at Nick each time he managed to locate himself in her way. She let physical action work upon her anger so completely that she didn't consciously hear the knock upon the door, yet turned to face the figure that strode into the room without bothering to knock twice.

'What the hell are you doing now?'

Alix was momentarily stunned. How could he possibly have the nerve to walk into her home as if he owned the place? Then the incongruity of that thought struck her, and she was forced to subdue the chuckle that struggled up through her anger. Of course . . . he *did* own it. Then anger took over, a slow, white-hot, cold-as-ice anger that flowed and ebbed through every nerve.

'I'm baking a cake, obviously,' she retorted scornfully. 'Get out!'

One dark eyebrow raised in a gesture that was so mockingly complacent she shivered in frustrated rage, but Quinn Tennant said nothing. He just stood there. Looking at her.

'I said get out. Out . . . out . . . out!' Alix's voice raised itself into a scream that bordered upon hysteria, and her entire body trembled.

'You sure do get excited.' His words were softly spoken, almost a whisper. But they echoed in the room like thunder, beating upon Alix's ears and then falling away into a troubled silence.

They stood glaring at each other, and Alix was irrelevantly struck once again by the rugged, masculine handsomeness of this arrogant, self-assured personage. Her eyes seemed to be drawn by a will of their own, ranging from his heavy, downturned eyebrows across the strong chin and the muscular column of his throat. He had taken off his tie, revealing an expanse of tanned throat and chest where tight-curled, coffee brown hair poked through the V of the half-open shirt.

Standing there, legs slightly spread and arms folded across his chest, he looked every inch the totally self-controlled master of all he surveyed. Except that in this case he was surveying *her*. The thought was sobering.

'If you don't leave here this very instant I shall set my dog on you,' said Alix with a great deal more confidence than she felt.

Quinn Tennant laughed, and she was surprised at the depth and warmth of that laughter. It was so genuine, so full, that she almost joined in without thinking.

'Nick? He hasn't got a vicious bone in his body,' he chuckled, and on hearing his name the dog sprang from his prone position just inside the bedroom door and trotted over to sit politely in front of the arrogant intruder, one paw uplifted.

'Good boy, Nick,' Quinn muttered gently, reaching down to shake the proffered paw. 'Now run along outside and let your friend out for a run. That's a good lad.' And before Alix could stammer out a denial, Nick was gone and the door closed silently behind him.

'Now,' said Quinn, 'what's all this packing about? Surely you're not planning to deprive us of your company so soon?'

'I certainly am,' Alix snapped.

He grinned. 'Do you always let your temper win out over your better judgement?'

'Frankly, I don't feel it's any of your business,' Alix replied haughtily.

'Ah, but that's where you're wrong,' he replied suavely. 'How would it look if you decamped after only one day here? People would think I'd been assaulting you or something.'

'Too bad!' She snapped the reply at him and turned away, reaching over to fling one last book into a suitcase already over-filled.

'Mr Jennings went to a lot of trouble to find this place for you. He won't be pleased if you don't even give it a fair go.'

Alix said nothing; she shut her ears to him and reached for something else to put into the suitcase.

'Damn it, look at me when I'm talking to you,' Quinn Tennant growled, reaching out to grasp her shoulder and fling her round to face him.

Fingers clawed, Alix reached out for his eyes in a catlike gesture that almost succeeded. 'Take your hands off me!' she hissed.

Quinn Tennant spread his hands in a retreat, stepping back out of range. 'It's just that I can't bring myself to apologise to somebody behind their back,' he said with a wry grin.

Apologise? Alix didn't believe it for a minute. He had already refused to apologise, and she knew instinctively that Quinn Tennant wasn't the type of man to change his mind easily. Besides, what difference could it make? He had made it abundantly clear that her presence here didn't please him.

'Save your breath,' she grunted, starting to turn away but halting when his hand reached out again.

'Damn it, don't be so stroppy, woman!' he snarled. 'You have a right to be a little upset, but there's no reason for taking it to extremes.'

'Well, thank you very much, Mr Tennant,' Alix retorted. 'I'm so glad you've acknowledged my right to be a little upset. Now would you get it through your head that I'd be a lot *less* upset if you'd just get out of here?'

'But I've come to apologise.' He said it in a deliberate little-boy voice that under almost any other circumstances would have drawn at least a ghost of a smile from Alix for its very incongruity. She said nothing.

'My God, but you're an exasperating woman,' he growled, and just for an instant Alix thought he was going to turn around and storm out the door. But instead he shook himself like a dog coming out of water and then continued.

'My dear Miss McLean, may I sincerely apologise for

misjudging you, for accusing you of something you didn't
do, and in addition may I invite you to join me for dinner
this evening as a small recompense for my terrible manners
in this affair?'

It was pompous, and they both knew it. But his sincerity
was evident in his direct, piercing gaze, and with the sincerity was the clear statement that this was as far as he
would go. It was an apology, but this wasn't a man to
crawl or throw off his dignity in the making of it. Alix was
torn between the desire to laugh at the pomposity of it or
to fling the apology back in his face. She did neither.
Instead, she took several deep breaths to regain some
composure of her own. It was ridiculous to carry this fight
any farther.

She didn't really want to fight any more with Quinn
Tennant, and suddenly she realised that she didn't really
want to start looking for another place to live . . . certainly
not at this time on a Sunday evening. To fling it in his face
and remove herself from the cottage would be cutting off
her nose to spite her face, and with that realisation came a
subtle calming.

'I accept your apology,' she said slowly, 'but I must, I'm
afraid, reject the dinner invitation.'

'I think you should reconsider.'

'You what?' She could feel herself growing rigid all over
again at the audacity of it all.

'I think you should reconsider. In fact I insist upon it.'
Quinn kept his voice calm and cool, standing there without any obvious aggressiveness. 'Because the invitation is
not only mine, but Mrs Babcock's, and she's gone to a great
deal of trouble to make it a fitting welcome dinner for you.'

'I see,' said Alix, who didn't see at all. How could Mrs
Babcock have gone to all this trouble? Obviously it was a
spur-of-the-moment invitation from Quinn Tennant himself, and his housekeeper would be simply following his
orders.

It was as if Quinn was reading her mind. 'I was supposed to mention it to you at the trials this morning,' he
said, 'but we were . . . interrupted before I got the chance.
And I was on my way to invite you when I found Anna

loose, only somehow we never got on to the right speaking terms then either.'

'Somehow? It's very difficult to be on reasonable speaking terms with somebody who's shouting at you for something you didn't do,' Alix retorted hotly.

'For which I've already apologised, so let's not discuss it again, if you don't mind,' Quinn replied with suspicious calm. Alix could see then that he was holding himself under rigid control, and for a moment she almost thought of apologising herself for bringing it up again. Almost . . .

'And what about your . . . Miss Keir?' she said then. 'Somehow I don't see . . .'

'Miss Keir has nothing to do with it, although she'll be at dinner too,' he interrupted. 'I just drove her home to change, and now I think I'd best leave and give you the same opportunity. Shall we expect you at eight, then?'

His final remark was more a statement than a question, and before Alix could reply he was turning away to step out of the door. He closed it behind him without a farewell, and by the time Alix reached it, he was halfway across the yard and reaching down to caress the dogs as they trotted up to him.

The abruptness of his retreat had made any response impossible, and Alix turned back to sit herself at the kitchen table, wondering at the strange turn of events. Then she looked at her watch and decided that having been committed to the engagement she had better do something about getting ready.

She had just stepped from the shower and was standing naked in the bathroom doorway when a thunderous knock at the door made her gasp in alarm. What if he were to follow his earlier precedent and simply barge in? Alix shouted from where she stood, alert for any movement of the doorknob and ready for an instant leap back into the bathroom.

'Please don't come in! I'm not . . .'

'Decent?' The single word was followed by an audible chuckle. 'Don't worry, I won't decide that this is the ideal moment to collect on my rain check, although it well might be. I've just come to say that Nick's kennelled up beside Anna and I've put in food and water for both of them.'

'A . . . er . . . thank you,' Alix stammered, unsure just what might be the proper response. It seemed just a bit unusual that Quinn could take charge of her dog after creating such an unholy stink about her supposedly letting *his* out, but she wasn't disposed to start another argument in her present state of undress.

'Good. I'll come for you just before eight, then.' And he was gone. He hadn't bothered to wait for an answer, and Alix tiptoed to the window just in time to see him striding round the corner of the house with a cheery wave to the dogs as he passed them.

What a strange man, she thought. So volatile . . . warm one minute and icy cold the next. And some people accused women of being moody!

One of her father's more irreverent sayings sprang to life upon Alix's lips and she grinned at the naughty appropriateness of it.

'Up and down like a whore's petticoat,' she repeated, 'and I wonder how you'd like hearing yourself described in those terms, Mr high-and-mighty Tennant?'

Whereupon she stalked back into the bathroom and began drying her long hair with slow, sensuous sweeps of her blow-dry comb. At first she simply stood, slightly hipshot, relaxing in the warm breeze from the dryer as it swept through her hair. But then she was drawn, inexplicably, to a study of herself in the full-length mirror on the door. And to making idle comparisons between her own tall slenderness and that of Michelle Keir.

Alix was slightly taller, she realised after looking back at the afternoon's encounter. And certainly not so slim. Her breasts were small and high-set, yet indisputably balanced to the rest of her figure. Her slender waist gave way to a gentle swelling of hips that were infinitely more substantial than those of Michelle, who Alix considered in retrospect to be closer to skinny than slender.

Alix had the type of figure which looked perfect in jeans, with a protuberant bottom that was self-contained without the usual accompaniment of fat thighs. Michelle, while suave and svelt-looking in her dark trouser suit, was probably too slender to look her best in casual clothes.

'Those probably *were* her casual clothes,' Alix muttered almost enviously. That pants suit had been expensive.

Whereupon she was forced to give serious thought to her own attire for the evening, and she immediately regretted not having asked Quinn Tennant just *how* special the dinner was being considered. She debated for an instant trotting over to the house to find out, then decided it would be unnecessary. If he had planned something terribly formal, Alix somehow felt he would have warned her . . . and he hadn't.

Still, there was this Michelle woman to consider, and instinct told Alix that Michelle's concept of casual could be very broadly interpreted to mean the dark-haired woman would always stand out. Not that it mattered if Michelle intended to keep emphasising her claim on Quinn Tennant. Alix couldn't care less about that, she decided. But still, it would be nice to look . . . competitive, just for the sheer joy of it.

When her hair was dry, Alix turned to her meagre wardrobe with an unspoken thanks that serious decisions weren't going to be required. She only had one dress that was entirely suitable for the occasion, being classy enough to hit the top end of the casual bracket without being showy.

It was a tailored affair with cape sleeves under a wide yoke, and the tailoring was saved by the fabric, which was soft and warm-looking in heather colours of gentle pinks, purples, greens and blues, draping softly from the yoke to just below her knees. She called it her rainbow dress, both for the colours and the fact that it always made her feel . . . special . . . when she wore it.

She decided to wear her hair in a tidy chignon rather than leave it loose. If nothing else, the style added maturity and set off her own features to best advantage; with her hair down she tended to look quite young unless the clothes were exactly right for that style.

Chunky, soft pink earrings and bracelet, soft green suede shoes and bag completed the outfit, and with a quick look

in the mirror Alix decided she was quite acceptable. She
wore only a hint of pale eyeliner and mascara, knowing her
fresh complexion had more allure than any make-up could
achieve for her.

And she was early, which was no surprise since her
parents had firmly established in her mind that feminine
lateness might be chic, but it was poor manners at best.
With fifteen minutes to spare, Alix poured a glass of cold
white wine and sat relaxed in her single armchair to drink
it.

Having completed her toilette, she stared into the glass
and pondered the motives behind taking such care about
her appearance. It was one thing to pass it off as irrelevant
competition with Michelle Keir, but another thing entirely
to convince herself that she wasn't all that attracted to
Quinn Tennant herself. He might be arrogant and argumentative, but she couldn't deny his handsome masculinity. Much less the tingle his touch had roused in her
when he had stroked her shoulder earlier that day.

In some respects, she thought, it was a pity they always
managed to strike sparks off each other. The kiss he had
given her by the roadside held promises best not considered.

Living at such close proximity, she decided, could have
more potential for problems than anything else, especially
since Michelle Keir seemed firmly implanted in Quinn
Tennant's affections. She couldn't underestimate his obvious interest in herself, but it would be wise to remember
that it was purely a casual interest.

Alix didn't want even that much of a relationship, much
less anything serious. Her betrayal by Bruce still rankled,
and she felt indisposed to trust any man now, especially
one so self-assured as Quinn Tennant. Mr Tennant, she
decided, was probably all too used to having his own way,
and she felt just a touch uneasy at the casual way he'd
mentioned his 'rain check'. Did the man never forget?

But then why should he? She herself hadn't forgotten.
Nor was she likely to, since the prospect held a full measure
of pleasure and risk. It would be rather nice to be kissed by
him again, but Alix determined that if it were to happen it

would be *she* who picked the time and place.

Maybe even tonight, she thought, and giggled slightly at the suggestion. How could it possibly be tonight, with Michelle Keir on hand to protect her investment? Still . . .

She was spared further speculation by a soft knock at the door, and she opened it to find Quinn Tennant standing there. He was casually but expensively dressed in a cashmere sports jacket and complementary-toned slacks and tie. If this was any example, she thought immediately, her own outfit was just right, and she smiled a little at the comfort of the thought.

'Not only punctual, but happy as well,' he grinned. 'I'll have to invite you to dinner more often, Alix; it makes a most pleasant change from feuding.'

Alix . . . There was a subtle sensuality to the way he spoke it, and Alix felt a warm shiver flow through her. It was almost as if he had touched her, and she realised that he was appraising her dress with a look of genuine pleasure as well.

'Very nice,' he confirmed, and his eyes said it wasn't only the dress he was appreciating.

'Thank you,' Alix replied with unnecessary coolness as she strove the contain the butterflies that erupted into flight in her stomach. It was terribly unsettling to have this man turn her bones to water merely by speaking her name.

And more so by taking her arm gently as they walked round to the front of the house, pausing momentarily to speak to the dogs as they passed the kennels. Alix couldn't resist running her fingers over the latches, and she was disproportionately pleased to see the sudden glance of speculation the action provided from Quinn Tennant.

They entered the house into a massive, high-ceilinged hallway, from which Quinn directed her to a large, comfortable-looking lounge room. The furniture was expensive and obviously carefully chosen to complement the graciousness of the room, and it was noticeable that Quinn considered his house first of all as a home.

When Mrs Babcock entered the room a moment later it became obvious as well that the diminutive woman was far from being only the housekeeper.

'My dear, how lovely you look,' she said, flitting around the room to prepare their drinks and talking a mile a minute just as she had on their first meeting. Alix noticed that Quinn accepted the chatter with an amused tolerance, treating the older woman more like a mother than anything else.

They sipped at their drinks—Alix had voted to continue with white wine, while Quinn had whisky and Mrs Babcock chose a very dry sherry—and Alix was quite content to let Mrs Babcock carry the conversation. This, apparently, was the normal order of things in the household, as Quinn said little except to spur Mrs Babcock on.

He seemed, in fact, all too content to let her occupy Alix's attention while he spent his time overtly watching her. At first Alix felt vaguely uncomfortable under his scrutiny, but she gradually realised it wasn't an especially lustful assessment, but merely an interested one. Still, she was happy when a ring at the door announced the arrival of the final dinner guest.

Michelle Keir was dressed exactly to the standard Alix had expected. Her two-piece cheesecloth suit was in a soft off-white, bordered with brown and gold embroidery on the skirt, blouse bottom and sleeves. The top was blouson and long-sleeved, with ties at the neck left undone and dangling to reveal just enough bosom to be interesting, from a masculine viewpoint.

The outfit did a great deal to emphasise the woman's slender figure, and Alix was inwardly piqued to notice that Michelle's legs, while slender, were quite as shapely as her own.

'Quinn dear! Sorry I'm late, but my blessed car wouldn't start and I had to find a taxi,' she announced breathlessly and then carefully steered the conversation in a direction that ensured he would offer to drive her home. Hardly surprising, Alix thought as she awarded Michelle points for a clever opening gambit.

What was surprising was the way in which Michelle treated Mrs Babcock throughout the rather excellent dinner that followed. Had she merely attempted to monopolise Quinn, which Alix fully expected and didn't worry about, Alix could have coped easily. But Michelle's attitude towards the older woman held a constant note of . . . superiority? Or perhaps condescension? Nothing obvious, of course, but enough to create a tangible tension.

Mrs Babcock's normal cheeriness seemed to face slightly, and her chatter fell away from the instant Michelle entered the house. She doesn't like Michelle, Alix thought immediately, and her suspicion was confirmed by the obvious tension between the two women.

If Quinn noticed, he gave no sign of it, except to devote most of his attention to Michelle, leaving Mrs Babcock free to converse with Alix during dinner. Clearly the older woman's chatter was an attempt to cover a quite unnecessary nervousness, and Alix found herself liking Mrs Babcock more all the time.

Whatever her position in the household, Mrs Babcock had an openness and generosity that was exceptionally warming, and during their conversation Alix found her to be an intelligent and knowledgeable person. She treated Alix almost as a cosseted grandchild, and Quinn got much the same treatment, in many respects. Only with Michelle was there that distinct reserve, and Alix thought it was because the dark-haired woman clearly viewed Mrs Babcock as a rival for Quinn's attentiveness.

All up, it made for a slightly uncomfortable evening despite the sumptuous roast duckling and other delicacies, and Alix wasn't wholly disappointed when it was time to excuse herself. She did so like Mrs Babcock, and she found it increasingly difficult to conceal her own distaste for Michelle Keir's attitude.

Her offer to help with the washing up was vigorously refused. 'You certainly may *not* help clean up after your own welcoming dinner!' the housekeeper declared staunchly. The fact that Michelle made no offer to help at all was ignored, apparently, by everyone. Alix suspected privately that she, too, would have been refused, but only provided Mrs Babcock survived the shock of having received the offer at all.

Certainly Mrs Babcock seemed to relax a great deal when Quinn and Michelle departed, and she was quick to suggest that Alix stay on for one final glass of wine.

'I just cannot like that woman,' she sighed when the door was safely closed on their departure. 'I've tried and tried, but there's something . . . vixenish about her.'

Alix chuckled aloud at how close the comment came to her own assessment, but thought it might be prudent to avoid any prolonged discussion of the woman Quinn so obviously fancied.

'Oh, I think it's just that Mr Tennant so obviously thinks a great deal of you,' she replied gently. 'Miss . . . Keir is the type to see that as somewhat threatening, I think. She doesn't strike me as the type who likes to share.'

Mrs Babcock's laugh at that response was both loud and honestly given. 'My very word, she isn't,' the housekeeper replied. 'And I suppose I should be flattered, but I'm not. Just what Quinn sees in her, apart from what's obvious, I cannot imagine. Although it's clear enough what she sees in him.'

'You can hardly blame her for that,' Alix smiled.

'Oh, I don't blame her,' was the reply. 'It's just that sometimes I wonder if Quinn really sees her as she is. Which is silly, really, because he's the most astute judge of other people I've ever met. He's certainly very taken with you; I can see that.'

'I hadn't noticed,' Alix said drily, all too aware of the little thrill inside her that leaped at the words. It was a thrill that surrendered to lack of nourishment in the end, because Quinn still hadn't returned when Alix finally took her own leave. In fact it was some hours before he returned. Alix knew, because she was still awake and wondering to herself if thoughts of Quinn and Michelle Keir had anything to do with it.

Ridiculous, she thought, and fell asleep almost immediately after the arrival of his car announced his return.

CHAPTER FOUR

THE next morning began in panic and grew continuously worse. First, Alix awoke two hours later than she had planned. And if Nick hadn't come into the bedroom to wuffle-wuffle-wuffle his desire to be let out, Alix might well have been even later.

Thanking her lucky stars for having taken time to bring the big dog into the cottage the night before, Alix shooed him out into the yard and scurried into the shower.

She was expected at her new job at eight o'clock, and with barely an hour to prepare in she managed to slip in the shower, thus getting her hair damp and giving up fifteen minutes for a last-minute drying, rip a fingernail through her second-last pair of tights, forcing a five-minute search for the sole remaining ones, and forget where she'd seen the padlock.

It was the padlock that worried her most. After Quinn Tennant's tirade of the day before, she was resolved not to have Nick in the kennel without a lock to make triple sure he stayed there.

There wasn't time for breakfast; she had to fly out of the house, round up the eager, bouncing dog and forcibly insert him into the kennel beside Anna, slam the lock into place and dash for her car. She made it to the engineering works with only a scant minute to spare.

From the outside, it wasn't an overly impressive building, despite being tidier than many others in the industrial estate. Inside was a quite different story.

A large, comfortably-appointed lobby gave access to both the design and workshop areas, with the administrative offices opening off the lobby as well. Alix waited only a moment under the expectable scrutiny of the receptionist before a smiling Mr Jennings arrived to greet her with such enthusiasm that she felt genuinely welcome and began to relax for the first time that morning.

'First we'll have the two-bob tour,' he announced, and they set off on a marathon journey through every section of the works. Alix was introduced to dozens of people whose names she instantly forgot, shown a variety of equipment that confused her even further, and finally, thankfully, escorted to a small, well-lit design studio where most things, at least, were familiar.

'It's something of a bad morning, I'm afraid,' Mr Jennings told her then. 'I have some clients arriving in just a few minutes and the big boss seems to be late himself this morning. So if you don't mind I'll leave you here to potter about, and one of us will get back to you as soon as possible.'

There was nothing else for it, and although Alix found it a strange way to begin, she found herself alone with an excellent range of design equipment and drafting tools but not the slightest idea what she should be doing with them.

She was able to busy herself for a few minutes inspecting the work in progress, but boredom began to make severe inroads upon her confidence as half an hour passed without a single person entering the room. She just had to do something, she felt, or risk being a nervous wreck by the time the 'big boss' finally did arrive.

She moved to an empty draughting table and began idly doodling, letting her mind float as she stared at the slow building-up of lines and scribbles on the immaculate emptiness of the paper.

And she had it!

An hour later the trash can beside her table was littered with discarded sketches and she was deep in her work, oblivious to the time and with her earlier nervousness quite forgotten.

It was yet another hour before she had got the sketching to where she could be sure of her ground, but finally she could go to fresh paper and begin a more substantial design.

She was almost finished, and was fairly buzzing inside with a ridiculous sense of satisfaction at having solved the problem of the untrustworthy kennel latch, when the door of her studio swung open to bang angrily against the wall.

'What . . . what are you doing here?' Alix could only stare then, wide-eyed with surprise and confusion, as Quinn Tennant strode into the room and halted before her, his own eyes hard with anger.

'The key,' he said brusquely, holding out his hand in a gesture so abrupt that Alix flinched away from him. His anger was a vibrant, tangible aura that filled the room, and he seemed to loom above her with a threatening presence.

'I . . . what . . . I don't understand,' she finally stammered, her eyes lifting from his outstretched hand to meet eyes like frozen emeralds.

'Obviously!' He spat out the word with such deliberate contempt that Alix recoiled in fear. Then he sighed very heavily and let his hand fall to the side of the faded green coverall he wore. 'I . . . want . . . the . . . key. Is that clear enough for you, Miss McLean?'

'What key?' Alix replied, then shook herself back to a reasonable alertness. What was Quinn Tennant doing in such a garment? she wondered. And what was he doing here, of all places? And *what* key?

'My God, woman . . . are you totally stupid?' he raged. 'I want the key to that bloody great padlock you've slapped on my kennel door, of course. What key do you think I mean?'

'Oh, *that* key,' Alix replied, and then had to stifle a giggle at the ridiculous sound of her reply. 'But why do you want it?'

He shook both hands in the air in a gesture of frustration that Alix thought for an instant would end with his huge fingers clamped around her neck. The muscles of his neck throbbed with his anger and his jaw was clamped so tightly as he fought for control that he had difficulty getting out his next words.

'Because . . . because I would like to get my dog out of the kennel, Miss McLean,' he grated. 'Some day, perhaps, when I have a great deal more time and patience, I would also like to know what in the hell you locked her in there in the first place for, but right now I would just like her out of there. Now, please, will you just give me the key?'

'Your . . . dog . . .?' Alix replied, her lips forming the two words very slowly as her mind went back over her movements of earlier that morning. She hadn't locked Quinn's dog into the kennel; she'd put the lock on the gate of Nick's enclosure. Or *had* she?

'You don't mean . . .' Her eyes widened in apprehension. She couldn't have made such a mistake. She just couldn't . . . and yet she had.

'I *do* mean,' he replied in a deliberately sarcastic tone. 'Now will you give me the damned key? I'm already half an hour late.'

'But why do you want your dog at this time on a work day?' The words in her mind emerged aloud, and Alix recoiled in panic at the expression they caused on Quinn Tennant's already angry countenance.

'That, Miss McLean, is none of your damned business,' he shouted angrily. 'But if it will get you off your backside I'll tell you. I have a client—an important client—who's very involved in quail hunting. We were going quail hunting. We will *still* go quail hunting, if you ever condescend to give me the key so that I can get Anna out of that damned kennel. Is that a sufficient explanation? Now will you give me the key?'

Alix reached automatically for her purse, then snatched back her hand as memory rushed in with its own awful message.

'I . . . I . . . don't have it,' she whispered, cringing back from the look of total incredulity on his face.

'You *what*?'

'I don't have it. It's at home, I think.'

'I can only hope that by *home*, you mean my cottage,' he said, voice frighteningly soft. 'Although I wouldn't be much surprised if you told me you've left the key in Melbourne.'

'Well, of course I mean the cottage,' she snapped, suddenly angered by his overbearing attitude. 'Surely you don't think I'm so stupid that I'd lock my dog in a kennel with a padlock I don't have a key for?'

Quinn merely raised one eyebrow. 'That's a pretty bold

statement for somebody who doesn't even know her own dog,' he retorted.

'Don't be stupid,' she shot back. 'I was in rather a hurry this morning, that's all. And I wish you'd stop trying to make so much out of a simple mistake. Or haven't *you* ever made a mistake?'

'Not when it comes to telling the girls from the boys,' he replied with a mocking grin, 'and I can usually recognise my own dog. Okay, the key is in the cottage—or so you say. Shall we just go and get it, or would you prefer me to spend the rest of the day searching among your belongings. until I find it?'

'I would *not*!' Alix was justifiably indignant. The absolute nerve of the man! She felt a chilling inside her at the thought of Quinn Tennant inspecting her clothing, her books, her private papers—all on the excuse of looking for the dratted key.

'I suppose you think I'd snoop,' he said mischievously, and he was so right that Alix felt herself flushing an admission. Quinn's eyes roved boldly over her figure, as if assessing the underclothing beneath her simple office dress. His grin, then, was predatory. 'Would it bother you all that much if I discovered you wear lacy pink old-fashioned bloomers? It shouldn't, because nothing about you would surprise me all that much—except maybe an exhibition of common sense and logic. But if it's worrying you, Miss McLean, don't let it. Just tell me where the key is and I'll promise to leave your . . . bloomers . . . undisturbed.'

There was a sensual quality to his words and eyes that quickened Alix's pulse, but it served also to fan her own growing anger. 'I can imagine what your promise might be worth,' she snapped. 'But it doesn't matter in any event, because I don't know exactly where the key is. So you'll just have to wait until my lunch break, when I'd be more than happy to go home and find it for you.'

'Lunch break, hell! You'll go and find it *now*,' he replied, and there was a steel-like firmness about his words.

'But I can't,' said Alix. 'I can't just walk out of here in the middle of the morning . . . it's my first day here. Now look, Mr Tennant, I'm very sorry for what's happened, but

I am here to do a job, not to jump at your beck and call. I would be very happy if you'd just leave, before the manager comes back for me. Or would you *like* to have me in trouble on my first day here? Yes, I suppose that's exactly what you'd like, isn't it?'

His eyes belied his words. 'No, Miss McLean, that is not what I want, nor is it what I would like,' he replied with a terrible calm. 'All that I want is to get that key so that I can remove Anna from the effects of your shortsightedness. And if it's of any consolation, I can absolutely assure you that getting me that key will not get you in any trouble here.'

'Easy enough to say,' Alix replied. She could just imagine Mr Jennings' reaction to a request that she take off half of her first morning just to give this obstinate, overbearing man his dog. Quail hunting indeed! She was about to expand her objections when the door opened to admit Mr Jennings and another man Alix had never seen before.

'Ah, here you are, Quinn,' said Jennings. 'Have you had a chance to get Miss McLean started on anything special, because if not I thought she might have a go at . . .'

Alix didn't hear the rest. Her mind swirled at the awful reality of Mr Jennings' obvious subservience and the confirmation she read in Quinn's sparkling green eyes.

He was the boss. *He* was the ultimate authority to which she must answer in her new job. And her landlord. And . . . and . . . She staggered then, and might have fallen but for his strong hand on her arm. She tried to shake it off, feeling both foolish and ashamed without any real reason, but his clasp was like iron.

And he was laughing. Laughing with a mocking cruelty that slashed through Alix's final defences like a knife.

' I have one or two things for Alix to do before I turn her over to you,' he chuckled to the business manager, who looked from one to the other in obvious confusion. It was clear that Mr Jennings couldn't comprehend either Quinn Tennant's amusement or Alix's own pale silence. 'Now about that key, Alix . . .'

He drew out her name slowly, giving it a sensuous, personal quality that was like a physical caress pulsing up

Alix's spine. It made her knees go weak and she could feel her pulse beating more quickly.

'Whatever you say, Mr Tennant,' she replied softly, hoping her voice didn't reveal the shakiness inside her. How could this be happening? Was this hateful, domineering, beastly man going to be *everywhere* in her new life? Laughing at her, mocking her, and worse—able to reach inside her and touch at nerves and feelings and emotions like some master pianist at work? It was frightening to have him angry with her, frightening to find herself so intricately bound up in his affairs, his home, but nothing was so frightening as the effect he could have on her inner, most personal feelings.

'Listen, mate, we're going to have to give the shooting a miss,' interjected the strange third man in the room. 'I just got a call saying they want me back in Brisbane this afternoon, so I'll have to grab the two o'clock plane.'

He paused thoughtfully, and Alix noticed for the first time consciously that he, too, was dressed in drab overalls and heavy field boots.

'Back to Brisbane already? But you just got here this morning.' Quinn looked at his visitor with an expression that could have been either amusement or exasperation. Alix didn't dare examine it too closely.

The man shrugged. 'You know how it is. There are some decisions you just can't delegate.' Then he grinned at Alix and it was such an open, genuine smile that she couldn't help returning it. 'Don't let him roust on you too much, miss,' the man said. 'It was a mistake anybody could make, and from the look of things I should be thanking you for it, because otherwise we'd be totally out of touch at a time I'm just as glad they were able to reach me.'

'I have no intention of rousting on Miss McLean,' Quinn retorted. He had moved around to the front of Alix's draughting table as they had been talking, and now turned to face her with the almost completed latch sketch in his hand.

'I presume this is your work.' And she nodded. Quinn looked at the sketch again, then flung it down on the table in a gesture Alix couldn't quite comprehend. 'Will you have finished it by this afternoon?' he asked.

'Yes, I . . . I think so, unless . . .'

'Right,' he interrupted, turning away to his shooting friend. 'Come and I'll buy you a decent lunch to make up for the shooting we've missed. Than I'll pour you on the plane and we'll hope for better luck next time.'

He turned back to Alix just before they went through the doorway. 'Don't worry about the padlock problem now, since it can obviously wait until you get home tonight. But I really would like to see that design finished this afternoon.' It was a message both for Alix and for Mr Jennings, who had picked up the design and was looking at it curiously.

But all he said was 'very interesting,' before he replaced the paper and scurried after the other two men, closing the door quietly behind him.

The snick of it closing was a signal for Alix to slump into her chair, sighing with the relief that coursed through her. She felt exhausted, both physically and mentally, by the incredible occurrences of the morning. How could she possibly have locked Anna up instead of Nick? Even in retrospect it didn't seem possible, but obviously she had done exactly that.

And to find that Quinn Tennant was the 'big boss'— that was a revelation Alix could have done without. And why should he show such interest in her doodling? Surely even Quinn Tennant must realise she'd only been passing the time, but now . . .

She spent the remainder of the morning on the drawing, broke for a light lunch at the small restaurant in the nearby Sugarland shopping centre, and finished her final drawing and perspective of the latch just before three o'clock. It was, she thought, rather a good example of her work, but what significance it could have to Quinn Tennant she couldn't imagine. Personally she would have preferred to work on something relevant to his own company and its work.

She was forced to approach Mr Jennings during afternoon tea-break, both to announce that she had finished the drawing as ordered by Mr Tennant, and to seek something else to work on for the balance of the afternoon.

Fortunately, he had several perspectives that required work, but Alix had barely begun when a tall, slender woman of about forty-five entered the room to announce that she was Mr Tennant's secretary and that he would see Miss McLean immediately.

It was a command, not an invitation, and Alix hastened to follow the other woman through the maze of corridors to the executive suite. And awaiting her was a far different Quinn Tennant from the one who had been so angry with her earlier that day.

This Quinn was dressed tidily in a light brown, pin-striped business suit with a sparkling white shirt and re-latively subdued tie and pocket handkerchief. Heavy gold cufflinks set off the expanse of cuff that showed from be-neath the suit coat sleeves, and his casual, loafer-style shoes were both shiny and expensive.

He had risen from behind an enormous desk to greet her, looming above her as he approached and gestured for her to be seated.

'Not there,' he rasped as she was about to take a seat directly across the desk from his executive armchair. In-stead, he directed her towards the snug trio of less formal furniture in one corner of the large office, and Alix noticed as she took the proffered seat that her drawings were dis-played on the small coffee table before the studio chair in which Quinn reclined.

In growing bewilderment she refused his offer of coffee, and again when he switched to tea. She couldn't even reply when he suggested a drink, then. What kind of boss went around offering a new employee alcohol in the middle of the afternoon? It was obvious he was trying to allay her growing nervousness, but it seemed so unusual a treatment that Alix only grew more and more uncomfort-able.

'For God's sake, settle down. I'm not going to bite you,' he snarled after his secretary had brought his coffee and departed with a querying look at Alix. 'Quite the opposite, in fact. You are a most surprising young lady, Alix.'

What could she say to that? Fortunately he didn't give

her time to worry about replying. He had picked up her final drawing of the gate latch as she thought it could be reworked to avoid the problem of accidental opening, and was studying it intently.

'You worked this out since our . . . confrontation last night?'

'This morning, actually,' she replied.

'Why?' The question was brusque, yet his tone of voice showed a definite interest.

'Well . . . oh, I don't know,' she replied lamely. 'I had . . . nothing else to do, and after . . . last night . . .'

'Oh, stop being all modest and shy and . . . *stupid*!' he snapped. 'Nobody expects you to have worked your feet off on the first day here and I know very well it isn't your fault you had nothing else to do. What I want to know is why *this*?'

'I just thought that style of latch could be improved, that's all,' she replied, wondering just what he was getting at. All she'd done was slightly alter two aspects of the mechanism; it wasn't as if she'd designed something unique.

'And you just reckoned you could improve on a design that's patented world-wide, and that's been tried and proven over a number of years?' There was something in his voice now, but Alix couldn't read it accurately. Anger? No, but a sort of probing intensity. She thought about her drawings and wondered if she had made some utterly stupid mistake, then decided that no, she definitely had not.

'I think I did improve it, yes,' she replied then, very quietly and not entirely sure of herself.

'And you don't think you might have been being just a little presumptuous?'

Presumptuous? After all the problems the stupid thing had caused her? The total misunderstandings, the blame? 'No,' she replied adamantly, 'I don't think it was in the least presumptuous. If the thing had been designed right in the first place then Nick couldn't have opened it, could he? As it is, a child could open that gate just by leaning on it the right way.'

Quinn's eyes seemed to harden slightly, and Alix's new-found confidence flowed away from her. 'Besides,' she muttered almost under her breath, 'I don't think it makes any difference. It's only a stupid gate latch.'

'Stupid?' His voice rose as he looked at her with apparent astonishment and not a little contempt.

'Oh, look, I'm sorry,' Alix replied wearily. 'But I honestly just don't know what you're on about. I had nothing else to do and I was bored and I drew some improvements I thought would make it better. I was only doodling, and I just don't see why you think it's so important.'

And to her surprise, Quinn Tennant smiled at her—a broad, genuine, warm smile that seemed to light up his entire face. It was almost disconcerting to see such an abrupt transition.

'No, it's I who should be apologising,' he said then. 'And I do, because I should have realised you couldn't possibly understand.' He chuckled, a soft, generous sound that somehow made him almost entirely human but no less easy to understand. 'Stand up, please, Miss McLean.'

Alix did, casting him an apprehensive look as she rose gracefully. Quinn also reared up from his seat and stepped round to stand facing her directly and very, very close.

'Close your eyes,' he said softly, and Alix complied despite an inner voice screaming out cautions to her. Quinn was putting one hand into his suit coat pocket as she did so, and Alix wondered what could possibly be going on. She got her answer, or part of it, an instant later, when his lips brushed against hers in a gesture so incredibly chaste and gentle and non-sexual that she didn't even have a chance to recoil before it was ended.

'That was only to say thank you, Alix. It had nothing to do with my rain check,' he said with a grin. 'And this is also to say thank you.'

Alix stared at the paper he had handed her, her mind refusing to accept what she saw. A cheque, in her name, and for an amount she simply couldn't comprehend.

'Actually, I think you've made some sort of industrial

history,' Quinn was saying. 'Earning a healthy bonus before your first day at work was over, it must be some kind of a record.'

'A bonus? But . . . I'm sorry, I just don't understand,' Alix stammered. She stared from the cheque to his amused grin and back again. 'I can't have earned any bonus; I haven't done anything. And in any event, this is . . . too much.'

She thrust the cheque at him, only to have *him* recoil in a gesture that would have been funny under other circumstances. 'Hell, no!' he said vehemently. 'It might even turn out that it isn't enough. You've improved that latch design more than you realise, my girl, and as soon as we've altered our patents it could turn out to be a world-class seller.'

'Your patents? You mean that you . . .?'

'It was one of my first,' he replied without undue modesty. 'And my only excuse for not making it better is that last night's incident was the first—at least to my knowledge—to reveal the particular weakness you've so admirably corrected.'

He stepped back and looked down at her with an expression of amused contentment. 'Well, don't just stand there looking at it; you're supposed to say "Thank you, Quinn" and tuck it away to buy a new dress with.'

'Before I spent this much on a dress I'd want my head examined,' Alix mused half to herself. 'Look, I can't take this. I just can't. I mean, I really haven't earned it or anything; I was only doodling . . .'

'Well then, I'd hate to see you when you're working hard,' he replied with a grim smile. 'You'd break me. And stop being silly about this, because doodling or not, you *have* earned it. Now come on, give in graciously. All you have to do is smile and say thank you, very nicely.'

'You're sure?' Alix really didn't know whether he was being serious or not. The cheque was for an inordinate amount, and she was beginning to have the feeling he was only toying with her.

'Of course I'm sure. And it's no joke and the cheque won't bounce either,' he replied with a grin. 'And tomorrow you can go buy a new dress during your lunch break, and tomorrow night I'll take you to dinner so you can show it off.'

'Oh, but . . .'

'Oh, but . . . nothing! You will consider it in the nature of an order, Miss McLean. Now say thank you, Quinn, like a good little girl. Come on . . .'

And Alix did, whereupon he immediately dismissed her and returned to his own work, leaving Alix totally unable to concentrate during the short time left in her first and quite unbelievable day of work.

Nor did Quinn Tennant show up during Alix's hurried removal of the offending padlock that evening, which should have made her happy but somehow didn't quite manage it.

Her second day at the job couldn't have been more different from the first. She got up in plenty of time for her shower and a light breakfast, gave Nick a brief training session on the back lawn, and arrived at the office to find sufficient draughting work to keep her abundantly busy.

She managed to meet the various office staff once again, and apart from one or two catty remarks about her bonus—which seemed to be common knowledge—found them all to be agreeable and pleasant people. If Quinn Tennant handed out bonuses like that as a regular thing, Alix considered, it was no wonder his staff appeared happy, energetic and enthusiastic.

She drove to the Sugarland shopping centre at lunch and bypassed food in favour of the search for a dress that would suit both herself and the boss's orders. She had no intention of spending even the majority of the bonus on a single dress, and was mightily pleased to come up with a medium-length jersey creation that suited her to perfection. It was a simple dress, using the clinging habit of the material to achieve a style that was revealing without being gaudy. Best of all, the pale honey-green matched her eyes and her favourite pair of evening shoes, which meant she could save on accessories.

The rest of the money from her bonus cheque stayed in

her new bank account, which was now more healthy than it had ever been in her working life. And there it would stay, Alix vowed. She wasn't totally certain she would be able to cope with Quinn Tennant as both boss and landlord, and a road stake might be a wise idea.

Except that isn't really the reason at all, she told herself honestly while applying make-up early that evening. You fancy him a lot, and it's going to be that which causes the trouble, not any nonsense about landlords.

'Not so,' she said aloud to her mirror. 'And even if it were, where's the sense in it? He's already quite well occupied with that Michelle woman—and she's not one to give up easily.'

The silent and not-so-silent dialogue continued as Alix finished her preparations, but it resolved nothing at all except to make her just a shade wary of allowing Quinn Tennant to get too close to her mind during dinner.

He had picked her up right on time and took her on a leisurely tour of the district's sole scenic highlight, an extinct volcano called the Hummock. It was a few kilometres east of Bundaberg, rising from the flat coastal plain in an approved cone shape. But there was no sign of volcanic activity, which was fair enough considering the volcano had long since died before European settlement in Australia.

What remained was a hillock that provided a site for some of the city's most prestigious homes and a lookout on the very crest that allowed a magnificent scenic panorama—especially at night during cane-firing season.

Quinn had said very little on the drive to the crest of the Hummock, and when they left the Citroën to stroll across the small grassy park, he kept his silence but took Alix's arm to keep her from stumbling in her high heels.

Far to the south-west, a field fired earlier that evening glowed like the remains of an enormous square campfire, while some distance to the west another field was grudgingly giving up its fiery fury.

'Look there,' Quinn said suddenly, and Alix looked to see what appeared like tiny fireflies in the soft darkness. But as she watched, they sprang to life in a flickering pattern of brilliance as the edges of another field flared, and within seconds, it seemed, was consumed by the flames. The fire roared skyward, chasing the cloud of dark smoke that blotted out the stars before being dissipated by the on-shore breezes.

Another flared up, and yet another, until from the high vantage point of the Hummock it seemed as if the world was exploding into flame. Each separate field twinkled, flared into brilliance and then faded to dull coals and then renewed darkness, and it seemed as if Alix and Quinn were alone on the edge of a world gone mad. She shivered, then suddenly became aware of his arm around her shoulders and turned to face him.

His strong features were even stronger in the questionable light, and his eyes burned into hers with an intensity that was amplified by the reaching, flickering flames around them.

He was going to kiss her; and Alix knew she wasn't going to object, or even speak. When his lips moved down to claim her own with an unexpected softness, she felt herself moulding to meet him, her arms rising to clasp around his neck as his fingers closed along the lower curve of her spine.

Quinn's jacket was open, and through the thin softness of his silken shirt, the heat of his body encompassed her breasts, teasing the nipples to a rigid throbbing. His fingers pressed more firmly at her back, drawing her closer against the strength of his thighs as her own softly divided against the hardness of him.

Alix twined her fingers into the curls at the nape of his neck, not thinking, hardly breathing as the desire surged up within her body. She was dimly aware of his fingers exploring her back, her shoulders, and then sliding with skilled direction into the closure of her gown, reaching down to draw forth her breasts to meet his searching lips.

It was madness, but such a stirring, flaming madness that she could not resist it. His lips formed around her breasts, breathing into her a surge of desire such as she had never before experienced. His hands were everywhere, stroking, rousing, caressing, and she found his lips, finally, as they came to part her mouth in what could only be surrender.

Surrender! She recoiled then in a gesture so flimsy and futile it was almost silly. But it was enough to lay the magic of the spell Quinn had cast upon her, and her next movement was more decisive. His fingers released her grudgingly, but he made no solid attempt to halt her as she stepped away from him, reaching up with fingers that trembled almost beyond control to try and straighten her clothing.

Not a word was said, but by the time she had finished he was reaching out with a fresh-lit cigarette, and Alix took it because she didn't know what else to do. The first inhalation almost choked her, so ragged was her breathing, and her fingers were so unsteady she could barely hold the thing.

'You'll want to straighten up,' he said then with a strange, subdued calmness, almost cool as the wind that now surged up the sides of the Hummock. Alix looked up to meet his eyes, but she couldn't read them and didn't dare take the time to try. She threw down the cigarette and fled to the interior of the big car, fumbling into her handbag for make-up and applying it with shaking fingers while the man who had caused the disrepair stood silently smoking and gazing seaward.

When he joined her, finally, there was a casual arrogance about him, an aura that left Alix feeling somehow that it had been she who had transgressed, she who had been the aggressor.

They drove off in silence, each lost in thoughts that Alix, for her part, considered best kept private. Her body still throbbed to the wonderous music of this man's lust and her own, and she felt her softly swollen mouth with a tentative tongue-tip. The fires in the cane were nothing compared to the white-hot lava he had stirred within her, and she realised that he knew as well as she how close her surrender had actually been.

'I suppose you expect me to say I'm sorry,' he muttered, the words almost a whisper in the breeze that caressed Alix through the open window. 'I won't, you know. Because I'm not.'

'I'd hardly expect it,' she replied, not knowing herself exactly what she meant, but feeling obliged to say something.

'Are you? Sorry, I mean.'

It was an unexpected question. And even more unexpectedly difficult to answer. Alix was no child; she had been kissed before and enjoyed it and likely would have the experience again. But she had never before felt the surge of raw emotion that Quinn Tennant had raised within her, never felt the pending total abandon of willing surrender. And she could never dare to let him know that.

'What is there to be sorry about?' she replied with a coolness she certainly didn't feel. 'Or did you want a critique of your performance?'

'That was uncalled for,' he replied with an edge to his voice.

'Then so was what you said. One shouldn't do things one feels constrained to apologise for.'

'Miaw!' he replied with a grin that held little humour. 'Besides, I never said I was even thinking of apologising.'

'Well, you should have.'

'Why? I didn't get the impression you were being forced into anything against your will.'

'I wasn't . . . I mean, I . . .' She halted, totally confused and all too aware that he had led her into it deliberately.

'Personally, I enjoyed it immensely,' he said with a friendly chuckle. 'It's going to make that rain check eminently enjoyable.'

'I do wish you wouldn't keep bringing *that* up,' Alix replied hotly. 'And besides, I would have thought your latest performance was more than rain check enough. I certainly don't feel myself under any obligation.'

'Nor should you,' he replied glibly. 'But that performance, as you called it, had nothing whatsoever to do with my collecting on the rain check. I'm saving that for a better time and place.'

'I think you're expecting rather a lot,' she retorted. 'With that attitude I'm rather surprised you haven't found some ingenious way for me to repay your so-called bonus.'

The heavy car slid to a halt on the narrow bitumen road, stopping so quickly that Alix was thrown forward and would have struck the dashboard but for the seat belt and Quinn's huge hand on her shoulder.

'Now that,' he said grimly, 'is going too damned far. You will apologise.'

His eyes were dark coals in a face whitened by rage, and Alix realised that he was not only frighteningly angry, but quite justified in being so.

'I'm sorry,' she said. 'It wasn't called for and it was extremely rude and I apologise.'

Quinn didn't answer, but he released her shoulder and the car began to move, if somewhat slowly. Alix was conscious of his deep, regular breathing, and felt instinctively that he was seeking control of his emotions before speaking.

'I *am* sorry,' she said earnestly, and was rewarded with a wolfish grin from the driver, who finally broke his silence.

'All right,' he said. 'And now that it's settled may I say I like the dress you bought with the bonus—without getting my head snapped off?'

'You may indeed,' she said, suddenly more relaxed than she had been all evening. They both smiled then, and the mood of contentment continued as they reached the restaurant and went inside.

It wasn't until they had drinks before them and their dinner ordered that Quinn brought up the subject of the bonus again, and this time he wasn't seeking a fight, but information.

'I don't quite understand why you were so surprised at that bonus,' he said very seriously. 'Surely you must have gained similar credit for your work where you were before. And the designs you got awards for a year or so ago, they were excellent.'

Alix explained that her designing hadn't been significant to her work in an architectural office, since architecture wasn't something she had ever felt totally comfortable with. And then, to her own surprise, she found herself being skilfully drawn out about the designs Bruce had appropriated, and ultimately about the rise and fall of the romance itself.

Quinn's anger was evident in the rude language he used,

without apology, to describe what should be done to people like Bruce. 'And although I'd like to be able to tell you it'll all catch up with him some day, I shan't,' he said then. 'Unfortunately it doesn't work that way in the real world, and swine like that can go a long way on other people's talent, provided they're lucky enough or have enough gall.'

'It really isn't important any more,' Alix replied. 'It's over and done with now, and in some respects I suppose it's a small price to pay for learning.'

'Depends what you learned,' he replied grimly. 'And unfortunately it seems all you'd be likely to get out of that particular experience is a healthy wariness towards men in general.'

'And what's wrong with that?'

'It's a negative reaction, and for somebody like you—an essentially positive person—it isn't the best alternative,' he said seriously. 'I'd hate to see all that warmth and vitality dissipated by one lousy experience.'

'Thank you, I think.' It had sounded like a kind of compliment, but one Alix couldn't quite bring herself to totally accept. 'But aren't you making just a bit much of all this? I mean, I haven't exactly turned into a confirmed man-hater or anything. I'm just a little more cautious than I was before. Personally, I don't think it's all that important.'

'That's because you're not looking at it from my viewpoint,' he grinned. 'I'm not exactly enthralled at the idea of being tarred with the same brush as this Bruce . . . what was his full name, anyway?'

Alix told him without thinking, then wondered why he wanted to know and asked him. Quinn merely shrugged.

'Just assessing former competition,' he replied, and she bristled at the implications.

'I don't particularly enjoy being considered as some kind of raffle prize or something,' she said quite coldly, but Quinn only laughed.

'I wasn't thinking of a raffle, and well you know it,' he said. But the waitress arrived with their first course before he could expand on that statement, and even after the meal had ended Alix wasn't sure he had ever intended to expand on it.

Instead, he turned to conversation on much safer topics, and by the time they had finished their coffee and liqueurs Alix was more relaxed and . . . content than she had been in months. When he wasn't trying to provoke an emotional reaction from her, Quinn Tennant was an urbane, charming and quite worldly fellow. His jokes were sophisticated without being smutty, and more important—they were funny. Laughably funny, without taking their humour from other people's hurts or from sexual innuendo.

By the end of the evening, too, Alix had learned quite a bit that she wanted to know about Quinn's engineering operation, and realised that for him, it was only one of several widespread business interests.

And, she realised, he knew quite a bit about her. Perhaps much more than she had ever intended to reveal, but Quinn was a skilled inquisitor. He seemed honestly . . . interested.

But when they arrived back home, earlier than Alix would have expected, he made no attempt to resume his earlier lovemaking. It was, she decided later in bed, nicer that way. But just a little disappointing, somehow, and she drifted into sleep without figuring out exactly why.

CHAPTER FIVE

THE next few weeks passed in an almost dreamlike lassitude in which Alix lived only one day at a time, revelling in the subtropical climate, the job which provided her with a growing sense of fulfilment and the periodic presence of Quinn Tennant.

She did very little, outside of her work. A little quiet reading, a great deal of exercising both her own dog and Anna by walking the many district beaches, and very little conscious thinking about her own status and the impact of her dynamic landlord/employer upon it.

Quinn was a constant part of her life both at work and during the occasional morning or evening walk he shared with her and the two dogs. The fact that he was a model of circumspect behaviour and—outside the office—an unusually silent companion only seemed to enhance the rapport which Alix found increasingly enjoyable.

They walked, one Saturday morning, for miles up the long expanse of beach at Moore Park. They were on the beach with the dogs and far from human interruption long before the sun floated up from the sea to bathe the beach in a growing warmth. But although they were together, they were also apart; except for a smiling 'good morning', Quinn said not one word during the hours of their trek. And Alix was content with his silence, since it seemed to match her own need for shared solitude.

Most mornings she greeted the dawn alone, rising early to drive with one dog or both to a secluded area at the north end of the beach at Mon Repos, where hares abounded in the scrub-covered sand dunes and virtually no one came except at weekends.

In the evenings, she sometimes drove farther afield, to Moore Park, or the rugged coastline of black lava rock between Bargara and Elliott Heads.

Very occasionally, Quinn would accompany her in

person, and on one warm evening he sat with her on a high crest near Innes Park and explained the story of his illegitimacy, making an almost ribald fairytale from what Alix knew must have been a lonely, poignant childhood. He had come through his early life in a hard school, abandoned by his unmarried mother while still in nappies and thrust from orphanage to orphanage, foster-home to foster-home in a childhood where his own independent spirit and private distrusts caused as many problems as anything else.

Mrs Babcock had been one of his earliest teachers in secondary school, and his story implied rather than specified the mothering role the tiny woman had assumed over the years. Alix's own observations could fill in many of the details about the relationship between the tall, mature businessman and the one woman who seemed so obviously to have shaped his ideas and character.

The adult Quinn Tennant mixed a worldly cynicism and toughness with a well hidden tenderness and compassion that exposed itself in unexpected ways.

His employees faced constant high standards and often impossible deadlines, but were compensated by bonuses and time off that often far outweighed the work involved. Personal problems, especially where children were involved, always received a hearing that was objective and fair, and Alix wasn't surprised that most of Quinn's employees revered him.

His arrogance and temper were reserved, it seemed, for those he considered stable enough to cope with them, but he showed little patience with people who underrated their abilities, and Alix sometimes sensed that he was evaluating her own attitudes towards her work and her particular talents.

Certainly he encouraged her to try new ideas, to explore any aspect of the job which interested her. He was both mentor and enthusiastic supporter, and it was hardly surprising that her work became the centre of her existence during those first weeks of settling in a new life style.

But he couldn't, Alix hoped, realise just how significant his support was becoming—both inside the office and out of it. Since their dinner together, he had not laid a finger upon her in anything but companionship, had said no word that could be interpreted as any form of sexual or romantic approach. Yet when he took her hand to help her down from the high seats of his Range Rover, her entire body quivered with the surge of pleasure she felt. When he smiled, her heart leapt in response.

By the end of the first fortnight she was in love with him, despite her personal avowal that it simply couldn't be happening. And he didn't even notice.

It was, she decided, entirely her own fault. She had, after all, made her initial lack of interest totally clear, and now simple pride kept her from making any obvious advances herself. Especially in view of the continuing influence of Michelle Keir, who seemed to have no problems in gaining Quinn's attention.

Alix knew Quinn was seeing a good deal of the other woman. She was a frequent visitor to his home, and seemed able to time her attendance at dog obedience classes to match those infrequent occasions when Quinn was also present.

Alix attended faithfully. Thursday evenings and Sunday mornings became as regular a part of her routine as her morning runs with the dog. She enjoyed the regimen of advanced training with Nick and the easy familiarity of people whose interests were similar.

But she did not like Michelle. And those feelings were abundantly returned, although neither woman went out of her way to seek confrontation or involvement. They were, Alix decided, very like two strange dogs meeting on neutral ground—unwilling to fight but equally unwilling to give any advantage to the other.

Her own problem was easily recognisable; she was jealous. But Michelle didn't have any need to be jealous, yet she went out of her way to ensure that Alix was not only snubbed, but knew she was being snubbed. If it weren't for the growing clarity of her feelings towards Quinn Tennant, Alix would have considered Michelle's attitude more humorous than anything else, but being treated like a lovesick teenager by the sophisticated older woman created a growing feeling of uncertainty in Alix every time they chanced to meet.

And *he* never noticed. Although how he could ignore the tension between them Alix couldn't understand. Indeed, sometimes he almost seemed to deliberately throw them together, just to see the sparks fly.

Michelle obviously enjoyed any opportunity to lord it over Alix, but Alix quickly found herself growing mightily sick of the game. The final straw was the start of the August school holidays and the obedience club's regular 'Fred Bassett' school for children.

It was a feature aimed at both promoting the club's image and at trying to help children with dogs to learn better control of their pets and the rudiments of obedience work. And for reasons Alix didn't bother to try and understand, it was Michelle's pet project, which made it comforting to know that she herself would be too involved in her own work to devote time to an extra-curricular project during working hours.

Only Quinn had other ideas.

'I won't do it,' was Alix's initial reaction when he called her into his office a few days before the class began and coolly informed her that she had been 'volunteered' to help out.

'What do you mean you won't do it? Of course you'll do it,' he replied with a stern arrogance that served only to make Alix even angrier.

How could he dare to simply volunteer her like this? And for something which would gain nothing but increased kudos for Michelle—probably at Alix's expense.

'I'm very sorry, but I meant what I said,' Alix replied. 'I'm not qualified for such a thing, and besides, I have quite enough on my plate right here. Or hadn't you noticed?'

'I notice everything that goes on in this office,' he replied sharply. 'But since I'm the one who pays you, I think it's only fair that I be the one who decides what you do with the time I'm paying for. And frankly I can't imagine why you're objecting. You like children, you like dogs, and a couple of hours every weekday afternoon isn't going to harm your work in the slightest.'

But I don't like your girl-friend and I'd sooner have nothing to do with any project she's in charge of, Alix thought, although she didn't say it. Instead, she hedged around the issue with several other objections, all of which were blithely and then firmly ignored.

'Look, I have no intention of arguing about this,' he replied finally. 'It's costing you nothing, it helps the club, and you're going to do it if I have to drag you down there every day by the scruff of the neck. It's about time you started to put your obedience training to some practical use anyway.'

'And just what is that supposed to mean?' Alix replied hotly.

'It means just what I said,' he retorted. 'Think about it, woman. You've got a first-class gun-dog—or could have—and what do you do with him? You puddle around twice a week doing regimented exercises and bore the poor animal half to death. He's a hunting dog, or would be if he ever had a chance.'

'And just what does that have to do with me being conscripted to help your girl-friend with her pet project?' Alix demanded angrily. 'It strikes me that you're getting into an issue that's purely none of your business.'

'None of my business, maybe.' Quinn was stolidly firm and unsmiling. 'But I meant what I said about Nick. It gives me the absolute pips to see a potentially good working dog treated like a toy.'

'You're . . . insufferable! It's absolutely none of your business if I choose to hunt with Nick, and you know it. But I suppose that's why you flunked him in the trial—because you think he should be out 'chasing quail or something instead of working in obedience?'

'I did not! I flunked him because he broke his stay, and you, dear Miss McLean, know that very well indeed. All I'm saying is that he was bred to be a gun-dog and he should have the chance to work as a gun-dog, not a bloody lapdog. Or haven't you even bothered to notice how often he points birds when you're walking out?'

'Of course I've noticed it, but it has nothing to do with what we're discussing,' Alix shouted. 'Nick is perfectly well

trained both as a pointer and a retriever, I'll have you
know—and neither has anything to do with training children in how to handle their dogs.'

'That big sook a proper gun-dog? Oh, come now, Miss
McLean. I may look gullible, but I know more about dogs
than that,' he replied with a harsh laugh.

'You're worse than gullible, you're chauvinistic and
blind and a little stupid as well,' Alix snapped, 'and you
still haven't explained what Nick hunting or not hunting
has to do with this stupid idea you have of me teaching at
the kiddies' obedience school.'

Quinn drew a deep breath, an action which brought his
massive throat muscles into bold relief above the neat knot
of his tie. 'All right, Miss McLean, let me clarify it,' he
retorted. 'What I'm saying is this: you've spent a great deal
of time working your dog in obedience. You do it well. You
have ignored, obviously, his potential in the work he was
bred for—which I might remind you is hunting, not playing silly games on the trials circuit, but that is neither here
nor there. What I'm saying is that you have a reasonable
empathy with children, you like dogs, and you should
think it rather generous of me to volunteer you to help both
by helping out at the Fred Bassett school. Actually, I
thought you'd be pleased to help, but I see I was wrong in
that regard. Too bad! Because you're going to help, whether you like it or not. That is an order to you from your
employer, Miss McLean, and you will obey it.'

'And if I don't?'

'If you don't, I shall very likely be extremely disappointed in you, and I shall be very angry with you, and I
shall make you regret it deeply. Is that clear?'

'It's perfectly clear,' Alix replied with a calm that surprised her.

Then she squared her shoulders and lowered her voice a
notch as she faced him with her ultimatum. 'But I would
like it clearly understood that I don't like your insinuations
about my dog, who is every bit as good a hunter as your
dog, *Mr* Tennant. And what's more I fully expect you to
apologise for your snide remarks. You may think that
hunting is the be-all and end-all of a G.S.P.'s existence, but

I happen to think differently, and I think *my* dog would agree with me. At least he's only confined to a kennel when it's absolutely necessary, which is more than can be said for some poor dogs I know.'

Which was a low blow and Alix knew it, because she knew very well that Quinn spent almost as much time with his own dog as she did with Nick, except that Anna didn't sleep in the house. But she was so angry, and so frustrated at being unable to avoid his order to help Michelle and thus lay herself open to pettiness and sniping that she really didn't need, that she used every weapon available.

'And besides,' she concluded with a confidence she didn't feel, 'I don't know how you can say Nick isn't a good hunter. You've never seen him hunt.'

'Well, that's easily enough arranged,' he said with a smirk Alix had already come to realise meant trouble. 'We're holding a combined utility trial and non-slip retrieving trial in a couple of weeks. Shall I enter him for you . . . and we'll see just how good a hunter he really is?'

'By all means,' she retorted. And when she saw the look of smug satisfaction in his eye she laughed inwardly with a smugness of her own—and thanked her lucky stars she had never revealed to the autocratic Quinn Tennant that Nick had gone hunting with her since he was three months old, was an accomplished retriever, and that she herself was a better-than-average shot. Why mention it now? It would be only that much more satisfactory for Quinn Tennant to find out, when the time was right, that her father had been a good enough hunter to train his daughter and his dogs to also enjoy the sport.

Fair enough, Nick had never been involved in proper, organised field trials. Nor had Alix, but she had been shooting quail and ducks since she was old enough to hold up a twelve-bore shotgun, and she had worked with dogs under her father's careful guidance long before Nick had come along.

And, what Quinn didn't know, was that Nick was perhaps the best gun-dog she had ever worked with, better by far than the various labrador retrievers that her father had trained before eventually switching to German Shorthaired Pointers after their first introduction to Australia.

Oh, how she longed to lash out at Quinn Tennant—to tell him to look at Anna's pedigree, which she had seen, and to tell him that her grandparents on both sides had been bred in her father's own kennels. That would make him sit up and take notice!

But she wouldn't . . . not now. Far better to wait until these wretched trials and then make him eat his words. Not that it would do the slightest bit of good with the first problem . . .

'Not that any of this alters my decision about your helping with the Fred Bassett school, of course,' Quinn said then.

'Oh no, of course not,' Alix replied. 'But I do wish you'd understand that I don't object to *helping* with the school; it's just that I don't like being *ordered* to do it.'

'Fair enough. I therefore rescind the order,' he said with a grin. 'My dear Alix, would you please, as a favour to me and to the other members of the organising committee, agree to lend us your wisdom and experience to help instruct the children involved in this school?'

It was smarmy and deliberately so, but it was a distinct withdrawal from his early autocratic attitude. 'Of course,' Alix replied with saccharine sweetness. 'I'd be very happy to help, and thank you for giving me the time off to do so.'

And she left Quinn's office with a slight feeling of having resolved the issue with at least some saving of face. Not that it made her any more pleased at being delegated to help Michelle build up her own image in Quinn's eyes, and when Alix reported at the Lions' Park below the main city traffic bridge for the first session of the Fred Bassett School, she found her worst fears immediately justified.

Michelle, looking quite resplendent in a fiery orange jumpsuit that was far too expensive for the job at hand, made it abundantly clear to Alix and the other helpers that she intended only to fill an executive role.

It was no surprise indeed when she drew Alix aside before the sessions began to say, 'Personally I'm very glad Quinn volunteered you for this little job, Alix. I'm sure you're very good with children, and I, quite frankly, can't abide the little horrors. Yeeeech! And look at all these scruffy mongrels they've brought with them. I shouldn't get too close to any of them, or you'll find yourself taking entire families of fleas and things home with you.'

Michelle's concept of herself as merely an administrator fell through, however, as the appointed hour approached and the children with their dogs just kept on arriving. Where fewer than a hundred children had been expected, there were now several dozen more than that, and Michelle had no choice but to take a hand herself.

Alix had to stifle a giggle when a monstrous, shaggy animal of questionable parentage introduced himself to Michelle by planting enormous muddy paws on her bosom, almost knocking the woman to the ground. But she had her own share of difficulties, as did all the volunteers, with the sheer numbers of children and dogs.

In theory it was relatively simple. The children were to be taught basic obedience work—how to train their dogs to behave reasonably well on a leash, to make them sit and accept the rudiments of heeling and simple control. In practice it was less simple, but within a few minutes Alix was happily involved and rather enjoying herself.

This first day would be the worst, she knew. By the third day they would have lost several young dog owners to more exciting holiday activities, leaving only those with a definite and sincere interest. But first she would have to get them through the initial class without undue difficulty.

Theoretically, the youngest of the would-be handlers was ten years of age, but Alix strongly suspected there were a few who wouldn't see that decade mark for a year or so, and she had most of the younger ones in her group. Michelle had chosen the oldest stratum of the flock, and had spent the first ten minutes of her session playing up her sergeant-major role, much to the amusement of her young charges and the other instructors.

Towards the end of the first day's session, the youngsters and their dogs were moving along well together, bar the expected few who had no conception of the word discipline. Alix's crew, perhaps because of being somewhat younger, were more amenable to the instruction, and she was justifiably pleased at that. It was less easy for Michelle, and a casual glance at her class caused Alix to suck in her breath as the two groups marched nearer to each other.

Leading Michelle's group was a tall, scrubby-looking youth with a bull terrier whose vicious eye had caught Alix's attention. He was eyeing every other dog with a look that spelled trouble, and Alix called across to Michelle before the two groups got too close.

'Better keep an eye on that fellow. He looks to be just spoiling for a fight.' And Alix veered her class just far enough away to avoid getting too close to the bull terrier and his evil glance.

'You just worry about your own group, if you don't mind,' Michelle snapped in return, and Alix looked back in horror to see the other woman directing her group even closer to the next one in line.

There was nothing Alix could do about it; she knew the other volunteers had heard the exchange or were equally aware of the bull terrier's pugnacious attitude, but nobody had even as much control of Michelle as the young lout sneeringly maintained on his stout little dog. The bull terrier would be given every chance to display his inherent fighting abilities, Alix feared, and his young master would probably only laugh.

Two minutes later her worst suspicions were confirmed. The last young handler in Alix's class was a slender, diminutive child with an enormous dog which he had shyly told her was a cross between an Irish Setter and a Dobermann Pinscher. Rusty was aptly named for his colour, and despite his size he was a quiet, extremely well-mannered animal. With his setter colouring and short, tidy coat, he was also an attractive dog despite his non-specific breeding.

He was also a full-grown male, adult dog, as was the bull terrier, and Alix realised too late that Michelle was not one to miss such an obvious potential for trouble.

Alix's back was turned when the terrier, apparently without warning, made a sudden leap at Rusty, clamping his enormous jaw on the other dog's ear. She turned at the squeal of alarm from the red dog and the cry of anger and fear from his young handler, and fought her way through the growing throng of young people and their dogs until she could reach the centre of the action.

The fight was already over; the bull terrier had been pulled away by his owner, who stood smirking his reflected superiority and almost daring anybody to object. But Rusty was shrieking his anger and hurt, and Alix knelt beside his weeping owner to find that the big dog was missing a small nick from one droopy ear.

She reached out for the dog's choke-chain collar, speaking softly to try and soothe him. Every time he shook his great head, spatters of blood flicked over Alix and the young lad, but she saw immediately the wound wasn't too serious in itself. The real problem would be in the undisciplined crowding of observers; the bull terrier was growling ominously and eyeing the throng in search of a fresh victim, and Alix stood up long enough to call on the other volunteers to disperse the young people and for somebody to bring the first-aid kit from her car.

'I have one here,' growled a familiar voice beside her, and she found Quinn Tennant kneeling to personally inspect the damage. Behind him, a slightly mocking grin on her face, stood Michelle, conveniently out of range of the blood which had already ruined Alix's blouse and jeans.

'Really, Alix . . . I did warn you about getting too close to that bull terrier,' she hissed, and Alix looked up in shock at the woman's deliberate two-faced lie. Then she was being pushed aside by Quinn, who shot her a furious glance as he struggled to stem the flow of blood from the dog's ear.

'. . . really thought she'd know better, Quinn darling,' Michelle was crooning witch-fashion, and Alix felt the words drumming into her numbed brain. '. . . don't know why you couldn't have sent somebody just a bit more experienced . . . shocking lack of responsibility . . . sure the parents . . .'

Alix thrust herself to her feet. She couldn't bear to hear any more of this, she thought. But how could she oppose such a deliberately malicious attack? Already Quinn had

lifted the dog and was carrying it to his Range Rover with
the young owner following behind him. That single look
had told her he thought it totally her fault, and nothing she
could say would change his mind, that was certain.

Fighting back her exasperated tears, she joined the
other instructors in the task of dismissing the youngsters
and ensuring they knew the time and requirements for the
next day's session. Quinn drove off with Rusty and his
master, presumably to the vet, and Alix noticed a smug
Michelle ensconced in the front passenger seat.

'See you tomorrow,' one of the other club members
shouted with a head-shaking gesture of sympathy, and Alix
nodded a reply that was far more certain than she felt. It
wasn't likely, she thought, that she'd be there the next day
at all.

When she got home, it took her some time to soak the
blood stains from her blouse and jeans, but once that was
done she was able to take a long shower and reflect on the
incident with a bit more perspective. She cooked herself a
light dinner and then walked Nick until almost dark, but
there was still no sign of Quinn.

She would watch for his return, and when he arrived she
would attempt some explanation, she decided. Not that
there was any real sense in trying to offset Michelle's mis-
chief, but at least she could find out how Rusty had fared.
It took until nine o'clock before she saw the approaching
car lights that signified Quinn's return, and Alix, herself
clean and fresh in a change of clothing, wondered if he had
spent all this time in the bloodstained suit he had been
wearing when she saw him last.

She presented herself at the door, trembling with a nervousness she couldn't bother to conceal, and when it opened
to reveal a stern-looking Quinn, Alix blurted out her
reason for being there.

'I just came . . . is . . . is the dog all right?' she stammered, almost cowering beneath his hard-eyed gaze.

'He'll survive,' was the chilling response, and Quinn
stepped back as if to close the door.

Alix squared her shoulders; she was determined to at
least have a try at explaining.

'It . . . shouldn't have happened, I know . . .' she began, only to be cut off.

'It certainly should not!'

'Well, it wasn't my fault,' Alix snapped, her control shattered by his icy response. Then she looked up to see, behind him, the unmistakable sheen of glossy dark hair and a wicked, foxy grin. Michelle was here! Blindly, Alix turned away, ignoring Quinn's response.

Breaking into a tear-blurred, panicky run, she rounded the corner of the house and sped past the kennels to the questionable sanctuary of her cottage.

It wasn't until much later, when she lay awake and fretful, her sleep stolen by the trauma of the afternoon, that memory recalled his words. And then only spasmodically.

Had he said, 'Oh . . . no,' in a typically scathing voice, or had it been 'I know?' Alix pondered that for some time, but she was asleep before her shattered composure could regain enough solidarity to try and work out the problem. And in the morning she was no closer to being sure.

She went to work expecting some opportunity to speak to Quinn without Michelle's interfering presence, but he apparently was either away from the office or deliberately unavailable throughout the day. When it came time for Alix to slip home and change for the dog school, she hesitated only briefly before deciding to continue with her 'volunteer' duties.

'And to hell with you if you don't like it,' she cursed aloud as she thrust herself into jeans and a T-shirt before driving away to begin another session with the children and Michelle.

Damned Michelle . . . sneaky, cunning, devious, lying Michelle. Well, let her just try anything today and I'll fix her! Alix vowed silently.

Fortunately, there was no need for quite so savage an attitude. Michelle was her usual conniving sweet self, but she was wise enough not to try and rub Alix's nose in the defeat of the day before.

Perhaps more important was the fact that the bull terrier wasn't there at all, and Rusty showed up with a rather complimentary bandage on his injured ear. Young Geoff, the dog's owner, was filled with praise at how Quinn Tennant had helped by driving them to the vet and then home to explain the accident to the child's mother.

'I told him it wasn't your fault, too, miss,' the child affirmed, but Alix determined that Quinn either hadn't heard or hadn't listened . . . probably hadn't believed it. Nothing else could explain his chilling attitude the night before, or was he prepared simply to accept his girl-friend's lies?

I don't care. I don't care . . . I don't care . . . I don't care, she told herself over and over, trying miserably to convince herself against the deep hurt inside that clamored aloud just how much she really did care. Even faced with the evidence, she couldn't quite make herself believe that Quinn could be so totally, inhumanly blind. Unless he was simply a different person entirely when around Michelle . . .

'Hallo, young Geoff. And how's Rusty? I see he doesn't seem to be suffering too awfully much.' Geoff's face lit up at the greeting, but Alix, several feet away, shivered miserably and tried to keep her attention on the rest of the class.

As a gesture, it was entirely wasted, because the class was over for the day anyway, and Alix found herself with little choice but to join Quinn and the boy in their inspection of Rusty's battle-scars. Before they could do more than exchange greetings, however, a silky voice announced the arrival of Michelle, and the end of any chance Alix might have to try and explain her position in the affair.

Quinn rose lithely to his feet as Geoff led the big dog away, and said to nobody in particular, 'The dog's well cared for. That ear should heal nicely, but I'm afraid he'll carry the scars to the end of his days.'

'Well, it's just as well he isn't a pure-bred dog, isn't it,' Michelle quipped. 'I mean, it hardly matters; he's just a mongrel.'

'I'm sure it matters damned well to young Geoff,' Alix snapped in reply, then turned on her heel and walked quickly away, her back rigid with suppressed anger but all too aware of Quinn Tennant's green eyes following her.

And the same to you, Quinn Tennant, she thought angrily. You deserve it!

The chilling attitude created by that afternoon carried on into the next day at work, and Alix found herself straining to keep her temper on the three occasions Quinn came into the studio to discuss her work. The dog incident wasn't brought up by him, and Alix was bothered if she'd be the first to raise it. Not after the attitude he had already shown.

Instead, she forced herself to be icily polite, dealing with the work problems calmly and professionally but giving Quinn no opportunity for non-essential small talk.

The next two days were easier, because Quinn was out of town, but conversely more difficult because Alix not only knew where he was—but with whom. And no matter how much she tried to convince herself that she didn't care anyway, the thought of Quinn enjoying the questionable delights of the annual Brisbane Show with Michelle did little for Alix's peace of mind.

Saturday morning, she knew, was to include the judging of gun-dogs and some working breeds, and by the time she rolled up at the office on Friday morning, she was more than half convinced she would fly to Brisbane next day to have a look. Except that *he* would be there, with Michelle, and Alix didn't feel confident enough to be sure of hiding her growing feelings for the man. Not that Quinn himself would ever have noticed, she thought. But Michelle . . . sneaky, lying, cunning Michelle . . . she would definitely notice something and speculate correctly.

She was just wrapping up her work before lunch when the telephone in her studio rang and she picked it up to hear an all-too-familiar voice.

'Glad I caught you,' Quinn's resonant voice said, and while Alix stood in dumbfounded amazement he rattled off a long list of instructions that amazed her even more.

In addition to collecting several 'important' papers, she was to carry them personally to Brisbane on that afternoon's two o'clock plane. Some of the papers related to design work she had been involved in, but Alix could see no relevance in the personal delivery of them. And she said so in terms so emphatically cold that even Quinn Tennant should have got the message.

'My dear Alix,' he said in tones that would brook no argument, 'has anybody ever told you that you have an alarming tendency to ignore the direct orders of your employer? Now stop it! Yours is not to reason why, etcetera, etcetera, etcetera . . . but to do what you're damned well told.'

He paused only slightly at her audible gasp of alarm at the long-distance chastisement. 'Now I want you on that plane without any further arguments. Bring the papers, enough clothing and feminine frippery to last you a day or two or three, make arrangements with Mrs B. to feed the dogs and all, and stop being obstreperous. It's unbecoming in a young woman.'

'Yes, Mr Tennant . . . anything you say, Mr Tennant,' she muttered, then almost dropped the phone when he fairly shouted through it:

'I heard that, and you may well wish I hadn't. Oh, and one final thing . . . you'd better bring that dress you bought with your bonus; you may need it.' Whereupon he hung up in her ear.

Alix didn't have time to rant and rage about the callous, domineering attitude he had shown. She had only just enough time, in fact, to throw together a travelling kit, make the arrangements he had requested, and taxi to the airport in time to make her plane.

Even on the short flight to Brisbane she was more intrigued than actually angry. What could be at the root of his demands? Would he explain when he met her at the airport? Or would he meet her at all? Quinn Tennant was more than capable, she knew, of simply leaving her a further round of terse instructions to await her as she got off the plane.

Despite the rush, she had found a moment to change into a casual but stylish dress that was slightly less businesslike than her usual office gear, and with hair piled high and just enough make-up, she didn't require the admiring glances of several male passengers to know she looked quite appetising indeed.

For what it was worth; there was no sign of Quinn

Tennant at the airport, only a message and a hired car to take her . . . where? The answer was revealed when the car stopped before a hotel of such luxury status that Alix would never personally have considered it. Surely Quinn didn't intend for her to stay here on company business, she mused as the driver took her cases inside and she followed to be directed by a smiling desk clerk to a suite high in the building.

She knocked tentatively at the door after dismissing the bell-boy, and immediately wished she had kept him with her. She felt quite ridiculous and suddenly all too vulnerable, standing suitcase in hand outside the door of this luxury suite. What could Quinn Tennant be thinking of?

Alix suddenly began having very deep misgivings about the whole thing, yet inwardly rejected any thoughts that Quinn had deliberately planned anything . . . no, he wouldn't. It simply wasn't his style.

'Alix! Right on time as usual,' he greeted her, ushering her into the room and stooping to collect her luggage almost in the same movement.

'You'll have a drink? Of course you will,' he grinned, 'and then I imagine you'll want to freshen up.'

'Somewhat bewildered, Alix allowed herself to be led across to where an ornate drinks cupboard held bottles, glasses and a small refrigerator. She said nothing as Quinn poured her drink, but perched precariously on the edge of the seat he offered and looked shyly into the glass.

'Here's to wicked weekends in the city,' he said, raising his glass with a flourish and treating Alix to a thoroughly wicked grin.

'My word,' she replied, suddenly confident again. He was having her on, playing out some deliberate charade of his own devising. But to what purpose? And did it matter anyway? She'd show him that two could play his silly little game, provided of course that it *was* a game . . .

'And is it?' The grin was gone but an unholy light lurked in those flashing green eyes.

'Is it what?' Alix replied innocently. Let him do all the work, she thought to herself. After all, I didn't start this.

'A game, of course. That's what you've been thinking.'

Alix merely shrugged.

'Of course it might not be,' he mused, almost as if he were talking to himself. 'Or do you totally discount the possibility of my bringing you here to seduce you into making mad, passionate love to me?'

'I'd think it a rather expensive waste of both our time if you did,' she replied calmly. 'But honestly, no. It isn't your style.'

He laughed, and Alix was relieved to see it was the kind of friendly, open laughter she had come to find one of the things she liked most about him. 'You flatter me ... I think,' Quinn said. 'Although I'm rather glad to see you consider me not entirely an ogre, even though you've been treating me rather like one lately.'

'I have not!'

'Oh? Sure could have fooled me. Or is this ice maiden image you've been portraying for the last few days the *real* Alix? If I didn't know you quite so well I'd almost believe it.'

'You don't know me at all,' she replied tartly. It gained only another, rather wicked, laugh.

'I know you far better than you think, Miss McLean,' he chuckled. 'Far better, and when I collect on my rain check I'll know you better still, but that'll have to wait on more pressing issues.'

He bent to pick up Alix's cases and walked ahead of her to a doorway opening to a most exquisite bedroom. 'Your own amenities,' he said, pointing to the en suite, 'and even a lock on the door, in case you're afraid of my good intentions vanishing during the night.'

'It's ... reassuring,' she replied cautiously, momentarily taken aback by the sheer luxury of the room. 'But surely you don't expect me to stay here ...'

'With me? Of course I do,' he replied with haughty calm. 'After all, dear girl, we are adults ... and, I hope, quite responsible adults. But if it worries you all that much ... I mean, I wouldn't want you wasting your weekend in mortal terror.'

'Responsible or not, there are still the proprieties,' Alix

replied, unsure of her ground and still not certain just how much of a game Quinn was playing. If she made too much of a fuss, she thought, he would be just as likely to inform her blandly that she was sharing the suite not with him, but with another woman. Another woman . . . like Michelle. That, she decided, would be just about par for the course.

'If you're implying I show something of a proprietorial interest in you, then you're quite correct,' he replied mockingly. 'After all, I have my investment to protect. Good rain checks are hard to come by these days.'

Alix couldn't help joining his laughter then, and when he suggested that she tidy up and then 'trundle off shopping or something until six o'clock at least,' she blithely accepted the suggestion without any further discussion.

When she had washed her face and unpacked her slender wardrobe, she returned somewhat apprehensively to the sitting room of the suite to find Quinn poring over the business papers she had brought. So intent was he that he failed to notice her arrival, and she took the moment to study him unseen.

In a casual but expensive suit, strong wrists protruding from French cuffs studded with heavy, simple gold cufflinks, he presented an impeccable image of the professional businessman, she decided. Only the slightly too long hair and bronzed suntan seemed slightly out of place, but Quinn Tennant need be no slave to imagery; he was his own man and all of a piece.

And when he suddenly looked up to find her watching him, it was Tennant the businessman, not Tennant the pseudo-lecher who spoke.

'Right, off you go, then,' he said rather brusquely. 'And please try to be back promptly at six, because we're dining at seven. You did bring your honey-coloured dress, I hope.'

Alix could only nod, slightly taken aback by the abrupt change in his demeanor. Of course she had brought the creamy golden-green dress; it was the nicest one she owned and her personal favourite, not least because of the pleasant mental associations involved. She couldn't, of course, tell Quinn how she had very nearly left it behind in strict defiance of his orders.

Then, as if suddenly becoming aware of her reaction to his brusqueness, he grinned and shook his head wearily. 'Sorry, Alix, I guess that sounded a bit short. It's just that the next couple of hours may be pretty hectic here and my mind sometimes gets extremely compartmentalised where business is concerned.'

He grinned again. 'Now trundle off and window-shop or something. I promise to be in a far better frame of mind when you return. Oh, and if you didn't bring anything comfortable for walking, pick up a pair of sneakers or something, because tomorrow we'll be spending most of the day at the Show, and I think you might find high heels a bit much.'

Alix took his advice, and also splurged on a pair of fashion jeans and a light cotton top to match. And she made certain to return promptly at six.

She was hailed by the desk clerk when she entered the lobby of the hotel, and mildly surprised to find that Mr Tennant was out, would return shortly, and would she please wait for him in the suite. What was the logic of sending her out if he wasn't using the suite himself in any event? she wondered, then decided it was none of her business and continued following Quinn's earlier instructions.

Dinner at seven ... then so be it. Alix took a leisurely shower, changed to her 'bonus' dress and spent more time than usual with her make-up and hair. Finally satisfied that she looked her very best, she returned to the sitting room and mixed herself a long, mild drink, then sat down with a magazine to await Quinn's return.

He didn't arrive until past six-thirty, and the evidence of strain showed clearly on his face when he finally strode through the door. But it was quickly replaced by an admiring smile as Alix rose to greet him.

'You look splendid,' he said sincerely. 'Now if you'll just pour me a good strong Scotch-and-water and don't say a single word for five minutes, I'll love you for ever.'

Alix raised one eyebrow enquiringly, but silently poured

him the drink and stood quiet as he strode over to stare
enigmatically out of the window as he sipped at the drink,
then gulped down the last half in a single swallow.

'Fantastic,' he muttered. 'Do it again while I get
changed, love, and then we'll be off.'

Alix shivered slightly at the implied domesticity of it all,
and when Quinn retired to his own bedroom to change for
dinner, she poured him another drink even stronger than
the first and then recklessly fixed herself one as well.

Damn all Australian men for their habit of calling every
woman 'love', she thought. Just the sound of it emerging
from his lips had made her go all quivery inside, and if
she'd dared to believe it meant anything at all . . . but no
sense thinking of that!

And yet she couldn't ignore just how comfortable it all
was, mixing his drinks, and now ultimately seeing him
emerge from the bedroom immaculate in dinner jacket
and dark trousers, his shoes gleaming and his hair slightly
kinky from the shower. His tie was a shade crooked, and
Alix's fingers quivered with a sudden desire to straighten it
for him . . . but too late, he had done it himself.

They finished their drinks in silence, Quinn thoughtful
and Alix suddenly unnerved by his proximity. Then they
were in the large hire car, driving the evening streets until
they arrived at the restaurant he had chosen.

Quinn's name brought instant attention from the head-
waiter, and they were immediately escorted to a large,
semi-private booth that to Alix's surprise was already
occupied. The two men there rose to greet her and Quinn,
and Alix stopped dead in her tracks, her heart rising into
her throat at the sight of the younger man.

It couldn't be, she thought. Bruce . . . here? For an
instant she feared she would faint; then anger surged forth
in salvation, only to be replaced by confusion as Quinn
spoke.

CHAPTER SIX

'This is the young lady whose designs you've been admiring, gentlemen—Alix McLean. Alix, please meet Dean Sanderson and his son Derek.'

At close quarters the startling resemblance between Derek Sanderson and Bruce was slightly less apparent, and when Derek spoke his greeting the Queensland twang of his accent was enough to destroy the myth almost entirely.

The men were, Alix discovered, exceptionally large clients of Quinn's various business interests, and indeed it was they who had taken up his time that afternoon.

Between Quinn and the older Sanderson there was an obvious atmosphere of comfortable competition and pleasure, but Alix sensed immediately that Quinn held the younger man in somewhat less regard. Not that it showed, especially, but there was . . . something . . . that spelled tension between them from the moment of her arrival with Quinn.

Alix half wished it had been as simple as jealousy, but she had been so surprised at the tall young Queenslander taking her hand and kissing it in the approved Continental fashion that she hadn't noticed Quinn's reaction to the gesture.

What was obvious, however, was that while Quinn and Dean Sanderson welcomed Alix's presence at what continued to be a business dinner, young Derek was far more impressed with her presence from a purely social viewpoint.

He courted her with undisguised vigour during the excellent dinner, allowing his father and Quinn to carry the business end of the conversation while he devoted himself exclusively to Alix and her needs.

It was, to say the very least, somewhat embarrassing. But there was nothing Alix could do to stave off the attention without being totally rude, and since *she* felt herself to be involved in the occasion only because of her business interest, she felt compelled to try and hold Derek at arm's length.

It was easier thought than done, especially when he was not speaking. Then, in certain movements of his head and a way he had of holding his mouth, he continued to be startlingly like Bruce. Enough so, in any event, that Alix found herself having to concentrate on not calling him Bruce.

And he was so young. Especially when compared to Quinn Tennant, who carried only a few years over Derek—and Bruce—in chronological age, but who was so totally, solidly self-assured that he seemed much older. It was a matter of maturity, Alix thought, and she found herself wondering what on earth she could ever have seen in Bruce in the first place.

I never loved him, not really, she thought. And coupled with that realisation and all its implications was the obvious confirmation that if she loved anyone, it was the enigmatic Quinn Tennant himself. Not, she considered, the wisest thing for her to do, but it was already done, and she could only begin planning how to ensure that he shouldn't find out.

At the moment that wasn't a problem. Quinn was deep in discussion with the older Sanderson, while young Derek . . .

'I'm sorry, but I missed that,' Alix was forced to say to Derek. 'Very rude of me, but my mind just . . . slipped away for a moment.'

'I should be terribly insulted, but I'll forgive you because you're so lovely,' he replied with the gallantry that was slowly becoming rather wearing. 'What I wanted to know was if you'd care to dance.'

Dance? Alix looked round the restaurant with fresh eyes, suddenly realising that it had a dance floor, and that obviously several other couples had been using it for some time.

'Yes. Yes, I would,' she replied then. And a few moments later she was sincerely regretting the impulsive reply. Derek's Continental manner, picked up during a three-month tour of Europe and nowhere near as suave as he imagined, obviously hadn't extended to any European dance floors.

Admittedly, the space in the restaurant was limited, but Derek didn't even need that excuse; he persisted in dancing as close to Alix as if they had been hemmed in by a crowd, and none of her gentle dissuaders had the slightest effect.

His strong arms held her against him as they moved around the floor, and she could feel his need of her despite the fact that it did nothing to rouse her own emotions. And finally, she could take no more. She forcibly thrust him away from her until she had gained breathing space, and specifically told him to please keep it that way.

'Ah, don't be so stuffy, Alix,' he replied. 'Or have you got something going with Tennant, and don't want me spoiling it?'

'I most certainly have not,' Alix replied honestly enough. She didn't add, but I wish I did have, and suspected young Sanderson wasn't astute enough to see it for himself. 'I simply don't enjoy dancing so closely, that's all,' she added.

'Well, I certainly do,' he replied, but for the rest of that dance he obeyed her wishes without further question and said nothing that required Alix to think a great deal before answering. And when they returned to the table, not before time, Alix personally reflected, Derek seemed to have abandoned some of the intensity of his attentions.

For that she was well and truly thankful, especially when Quinn broke off his conversation with the older Sanderson and himself asked her to dance.

'I'm sorry this developed into so much of a business evening,' he said once they were on the dance floor. 'I really didn't intend to have us stuck with the Sandersons at all, but there were one or two things that needed straightening out. And I must say you've been extremely helpful.'

'I really can't see how,' Alix replied truthfully. 'All I seem to have done is keep the son's mind off . . .' She halted, looking up to meet the laughter in his eyes. 'You planned it just that way, didn't you?' she asked then, and didn't really need his slow nod of reply.

'Actually, plan is a rather strong word,' Quinn said then. 'What I actually planned was for us to have dinner alone, but I can't deny that your ... diversion ... of Derek's interest has allowed me to conclude my business with his father a good deal more quickly.'

'I don't particularly fancy being used as a ... diversion,' Alix replied, shifting herself rigidly away from his encircling arms. 'There's something rather cheap about the implications.'

'Well, if so, I certainly apologise,' Quinn responded, 'because *that* was never intended. As a matter of fact I thought you rather enjoyed the young pup's attentions.'

'Not particularly,' Alix snapped.

'Who is it you know that he reminds you so much of?' Quinn asked, ignoring the icy tones in her voice as he continued to whirl her expertly around the small dance floor. 'Your ... former fiancé?'

'As a matter of fact, yes,' said Alix. 'Although I fail to see what difference that makes.'

'Humph! I would have thought your taste had matured somewhat by now,' he replied with stunning accuracy.

'And what makes you so certain it hasn't?' Alix asked.

He laughed, a low, guttural growl of a laugh. 'Well, I didn't notice you keeping him at arm's length when you were dancing.'

'Perhaps I had little choice.'

'Or perhaps you just liked it,' he said, and she looked up to meet eyes that seemed horribly cold.

'And what if I did?' she replied, in an about-face that surprised even herself. 'I fail to see why you should be complaining about it, since it so aptly served your purpose.'

'Who's complaining?' And then, after a pause that seemed hours long, 'Is he really that much like ... what's his name ... Bruce?'

'Only in appearance,' Alix replied. 'I could hardly imagine them being much alike otherwise.'

'They obviously fancy the same type in women,' he grinned, 'not that I'd hold that against them.'

Alix's heart thundered inside her breast so that it seemed to fill the room, and she was certain that Quinn must also be able to hear it. Or feel it through the soft materials that seemed only to transfer his body heat to her with a strange, burning intensity.

And then it was as if he had heard, because his arms tightened slowly to draw her against him, not with the impetuous passion that Derek had shown, but with an inexorable gentleness that Alix couldn't have resisted if she'd tried.

As if to his silent command, the music changed to a slow, rhythmic number that allowed them to drift like thistle-down around the small dance floor, and Alix was const-antly aware of the touch of his hand at her back, of his thigh moving against hers in the turns. And of the scent of him as her cheek snuggled close in against his chest.

It was a clean, heady fragrance, like heather and old wine, and it filled her being with a need for him that was almost frightening in its intensity.

She let her left hand curl around his neck, unconsciously toying with the shaggy hair as her cheek nestled against him. She seemed to flow against him, into him, melting in his close embrace as the music surrounded them, creating its own oblivion. She didn't want it to end, not ever; in-stead let her dance this way for ever in an unceasing dream of contentment.

Contentment quickly ended. 'Hey, don't go to sleep on me,' Quinn whispered into her ear, shifting so that they were again in a more or less conventional dance position.

Sleep? Was the man blind, she wondered . . . or just quite deliberately obtuse? She looked up to meet his sparkling green eyes, hoping desperately to find in them something of her own feelings, something of her own gentle contentment. No such thing; Quinn was already looking away, nodding his handsome head in response to some unseen signal from the Sandersons.

And then, damnably, he was guiding Alix back to their table, moving easily and without apparent regret from the magic wonderland she had found with him on the dance floor.

To her surprise, he was immediately Quinn Tennant the businessman, and when Alix heard him suggest that they all return to his suite for a nightcap, because he had some other drawings there that Sanderson senior wanted another look at, she could have wept her frustration.

On the drive back, she was a physical obstruction, seated between the older Sanderson and Quinn as they talked business in the hire car's rear seat, while Derek shared the front with the silent driver.

But once back at the suite, she was easily nudged into the somewhat more acceptable role of hostess, pouring the men's drinks and sitting quietly for the few minutes they devoted to a reassessment of the drawings. Mercifully, it didn't last long. The elder Sanderson indicated his intention to depart, and all three men rose in a body.

'May I see you to your room before I leave, Alix?' asked Derek then, and Alix, momentarily flustered by the request and the impossibility of an answer, could only look at him dumbly.

What to say? She was searching for a gracious refusal when Quinn's deep voice broke the silence.

'Certainly, Derek,' he replied quietly. 'It's right over there.' And he nodded towards the door to Alix's bedroom with a look that said far more than his words and implied even more yet.

Alix's blush of embarrassment very nearly matched the look of total incredulity on Derek's face, and she would have laughed at his expression but for the implications of Quinn's wicked, mocking grin.

'I . . . see,' Derek replied slowly. 'Well, in that case . . .' His voice trailed off as he moved towards the door with his father, who seemed inordinately amused by the whole thing. Derek paused at the door, then surprisingly reached over to take Alix's hand. 'Perhaps I'll see you at the Show tomorrow,' he whispered softly, then stepped away into the reverberating silence that heralded their departure.

Alix stood there, numbed by a pain that encapsulated her, as Quinn strolled over to pour them fresh drinks. How *could* he have done such a thing? It was as if she'd been clubbed, and her mind simply refused to accept the enormity of it all.

When Quinn returned to reach her glass towards her, Alix took it without thinking, her fingers closing spasmodically around the glass as if it were somehow a link with distant reality. Was she mistaken? But she couldn't be. This man, Quinn Tennant—this man she *loved*—had not only humiliated her beyond all belief, but now he was giving her a fresh drink as if nothing at all had happened.

And . . . he was laughing! Not out loud, but she could see the laughter bubbling in his green eyes, a mocking, horrid, evil laughter at the knowledge of what he had so deliberately done.

'He's persistent; you have to give him credit for that,' he said then, and Alix stood silently, almost seeing each word emerge to float in the air between them.

'I don't . . . believe this,' she whispered, not entirely sure that she had spoken aloud. Her eyes were locked on Quinn's and she held the glass like a lifeline. Quinn's eyebrows rose in question, but he didn't speak.

'You're . . . you're . . . *mad*!' she whispered, quite audibly this time. 'Worse than mad. You're absolutely hateful . . . evil . . . contemptible! No, you're beyond contempt.' Her eyes were wide with disbelief and welling with tears that threatened her vision.

Quinn's laugh was a bark, a harsh, resonant sound in the living stillness surrounding them.

'You must be more hung up on . . . Bruce than I thought,' he growled, 'if you get this upset at me putting young Sanderson in his place.'

'I couldn't give a damn for Bruce,' Alix snarled back. 'But you . . . you've made me look cheap . . . just to put Derek *in his place*? What . . . are . . . you?' Her voice climbed almost to a scream, then dropped away to the barest of whispers.

'Don't you think you're over-dramatising this?' Quinn asked, still standing, drink in hand, and looking totally calm and unruffled.

Alix stared down into her glass for an instant, then rage gave motion to her body. With a single flick of her wrist she flung the contents of the glass into his face as she screamed at him.

'Over-dramatising? I'll give you over-dramatising, you utter swine! Can't you understand plain English? You've made me look cheap and disgusting!'

Quinn recoiled only slightly, and instead of hardening with the anger she expected, his eyes took on a speculating expression. Then he reached out with one hand and cupped her chin, holding her face so that he could probe her eyes with his own.

Alix half raised her free hand to strike at him, but the gesture died stillborn as those eyes transfixed her. His fingers tightened slightly upon her chin, and then he was pulling her closer to him, pulling so slightly that the movement was a slow, barely noticeable act.

'No,' he said then, the word emerging as a slight whisper. 'No, Not cheap, and never, never disgusting. Only . . . very desirable . . .'

His lips followed the words down to take her mouth, then, effectively halting whatever retort might be forthcoming. The kiss was slow, deliberate, possessive. And demanding. His lips burned like a brand, and once his mouth had locked them together his hand slid from its capture of her chin to begin a light, feather-soft descent down the column of her throat. Each movement, each touch was a deliberate, sensuous assault upon the fragility of her emotions, and when his hand slid down to the hollow of her throat, the fingers of the other hand flexed like electric wires around the softness at the base of her spine.

Alix's mind was a kaleidoscope of emotions, loving him, hating him, whirling between enthralment and scarlet, freezing repulsion. But her body suffered no such confusion. When his fingers touched her breasts, the nipples roused themselves to meet the touch . . . when the rigid warmth of his masculinity seared through the clothing between them, her most intimate nerves cried out their submissiveness.

Quinn held her hard against him, their bodies moulding as his fingers stroked and caressed her from the feverish heat of her bare neck and shoulders to the swelling softness of her upper thighs. Her mind cried out against him, screaming its silent defiance of his expert lovemaking, shouting her hatred of him, whispering her love.

And her hips pressed against him with a pliant, need-driven boldness as her fingers laced about his neck, her lips joined his in the search for fulfilment. When his hands gently turned her so that he could free her breasts to the searing assault of his lips, she helped him and screamed inside for him to stop. When his searching fingers fumbled with the fastenings of the dress, she trembled and feared and kicked him in her mind, but her body stayed still and did nothing to hinder the progress of those fingers.

Her mind screamed out his name. Devil ... devil ... devil! But her lips whispered, 'Quinn ... Quinn,' against the tormenting exploration of his lips.

The dress slid from her shoulders, pausing only momentarily at her hips before his urging fingers thrust it down to fall in a crumpled heap around her feet. The half-slip followed it and she writhed with him as her bra relinquished heaving breasts to the attention of his lips.

But when his arm slid beneath her knees and he stooped to lift her, carrying her like a child to the doorway of his bedroom and through it, her mind took strength from the respite and she kicked out in fear and anger.

When he laid her down upon the vastness of the big double bed, she rolled across it and landed athletically on the floor beyond, turning to sprint for the doorway and the lighted area beyond.

Quinn caught her easily, turning her body back against him as he searched for her mouth with his lips, silent, and the more to be feared because of it. He was neither rough nor over-gentle, but his insistence and total expertise was beyond anything Alix could summon to combat it.

Again she felt the heat of him against her, and now there was so little between them that her body seemed to catch fire from his magic fingers and his searching, compelling mouth.

Alix's body trembled upon the brink of total surrender, but her mental strength surged upward to take a final, desperate stand.

'All right, Mr Tennant . . . take what you've paid for,' she gasped aloud, her body going rigid with the words. He would take her now, she was sure of it. But he would take only her body. Alix could not, would not allow him anything beyond that.

'Paid . . . for . . .?' The words escaped him in a slow, painful expulsion that revealed how far removed his active mind had been. And then he was no longer against her; his hands touched only her shoulders as he thrust her away so brutally that she almost fell.

His eyes burned like the green fires of hell as he stood, then, looking down at her with a contempt that sparked like lightning across the space between them. And he turned away, lurching through the doorway to his room, slamming the door behind him with a sound like the crack of doom.

Alix stood for a moment, trembling. Then, with a cry that poured up uncontrolled from her heart, she grabbed up her discarded clothing and fled to the questionable sanctuary of her own room.

Precipitous flight was the primary thought in her confused and shocked consciousness. Without even bothering to dress herself, she grabbed up the telephone and asked for a connection to the airline offices. There must be a flight. Now. Immediately.

But there was not. When she was finally connected a rather bored-sounding reservations clerk told her the next two flights would not be until later that morning; and they were booked solid. The first possible plane she could catch didn't leave until the afternoon.

Alix slammed down the telephone in a paroxysm of rage and shame. She couldn't stay! She simply couldn't. To have to face Quinn Tennant in the morning? Throwing on her robe, she began to toss clothing helter-skelter into her suitcase, oblivious to the wrinkling and mess that she created.

And then the tears started, welling from her eyes in a blinding torrent that prohibited any further action. How could she have allowed things to go so far? How could her body have betrayed her so wantonly . . . and worse, how could her rapier tongue have so viperishly assaulted Quinn for merely doing what both of them wanted?

Her pillow was saturated by the time she ceased crying, but her idea of instant flight had also dissipated. Where, indeed, could she flee to at three o'clock in the morning?

Even in the aftermath of the traumatic situation, Alix's body paid scant attention to the machinations of her mind. Where Quinn's lips had touched her, she tingled. Where his hateful-delightful fingers had caressed her, she could still feel the rousing pleasure of their touch. Her soft lips were swollen and over-sensitive; even the touch of her own tongue recalled the impelling touch of his. Never in her life had Alix's body been so aroused, and never had she felt so totally helpless . . . or so totally ashamed.

She was not *that* inexperienced. She should have been able to turn Quinn off without being forced to insult him so provocatively. Had she wanted to . . . but of course she had not. In retrospect Alix was forced to admit that her own desire had more than matched his, and if anything her control had been less.

Pushing her half-filled suitcase aside, she sprawled across the bed, head propped on the pillows, and relived the experience again and again in her mind. She formulated other words she might have said, other actions she might have taken. And she allowed herself, almost unwillingly, to speculate on what would have happened had she said nothing, merely allowed the flaring of their passions to burst into full-bodied, living fulfilment. And for a moment, at least, she wished it had happened.

Instead—what? A total destruction of everything. What must Quinn think of her? If anything. And worse, what would he think of her tomorrow . . . today? She fell asleep still wondering.

'Alix . . . breakfast in twenty minutes!'

She opened her sleep-smudged eyes with a start. Had it been . . . but it must have been Quinn speaking. Alix froze. Her mouth quivered, opened, closed. But nothing came out. She pushed herself partly upright and stared at the door where the fingers—his fingers—had knocked.

'Alix?' There was no anger in the voice, no contempt. Only a slight inflection of concern. 'You all right?'

'Y . . . y . . . yes,' she replied tentatively, surprised to hear the word actually emerge from her dry but still-tender lips.

'Right! Twenty minutes . . . or do you need more?'

'No . . . no, that's fine,' she replied cautiously. 'I'm just . . . what time is it?'

'Six-thirty.' Was there a hint of chuckle in that abrupt reply? He must be lying. Why in heaven's name would he waken her at such a ridiculous hour?

'Six . . . thirty?' she speaked, then lapsed into silence. The guilt she had gone to sleep with rose to fill her throat.

'That's what I said.' Definitely there was a throaty chuckle this time. 'Come on, girl. It's not all *that* early. And they start judging the dogs early, so get the lead out and hurry things up a bit or you'll miss half of it. And don't forget your walking shoes; I fancy you'll need them today.'

And he was gone. Alix knew it without being able to hear his departing footsteps on the thick carpeting of the suite.

She was ready in less than the twenty minutes, but she stayed in her room, dithering and growing increasingly nervous and increasingly angry with herself for being so, until he hammered on the door and announced, 'Breakfast is here. Are you ready?'

'Yes,' she replied resolutely, and after gathering her courage she flung open the door and stepped out to face her host.

Quinn looked up at her from his seat at the small dining table, then rose languidly to his feet and held out a chair for her. He was dressed in a casual outfit of snug-fitting denims and a light shirt that was open halfway down his chest to reveal a heavy gold chain nestled in the curling hair. The jeans halted just above a pair of soft, expensive leather walking boots. Alix only half noticed his clothing; her attention was on his ruggedly handsome face, searching vainly for some hint as to his mood.

But it was a waste. Those deep green eyes were pleasantly welcoming, he nodded a silent approval at her own clothing and sensible footwear, then motioned her into the chair he held.

The small table was loaded with platters. Steak and eggs, stacks of hot buttered toast, crumpets, sausages and bacon and various condiments vied for position with a huge pot of steaming coffee, another of tea, and the various cutlery.

'My . . . goodness!' Alix exclaimed involuntarily. Did he really expect just the two of them to eat all this? He couldn't possibly!

Quinn chuckled. 'Don't look at it—eat it,' he said quietly. 'Don't worry, you'll still have room for fairy-floss and whatever at the Show.'

Alix shook her head wonderingly. It didn't seem possible, but his words somehow created a surge of hunger inside her, and she quickly followed his example and began tucking into the food. Quinn ate quickly but with a contained neatness, and before Alix realised it the majority of the food was gone and he was reaching for the coffee pot.

'Or would you prefer tea?' he asked. 'I wasn't sure, so I ordered both.'

'Oh, no . . . coffee is fine,' Alix replied, forced to pause before answering because her mouth was full. She managed to nod her way through the expected questions about sugar and cream, but as both of them leaned back in their chairs for the supposedly relaxing interlude of after-breakfast coffee, her now full stomach began to knot up.

'I . . . er . . . about last night . . .' she began nervously.

'Forget it.' His voice was gentle, calm, yet edged with an iron she could feel.

Alix gathered her resolve. She could not . . . simply could *not* spend this day with Quinn without making some gesture of apology. She *must* not.

'I don't want to forget it,' she replied, and then, as he opened his mouth to halt her, she rushed out the words. 'Last night was . . . was . . . very beautiful . . . and I'm . . . I'm . . . sorry I said what I did . . .'

One dark eyebrow was raised enquiringly, but Quinn made no reply. He seemed only to settle more comfortably into his chair, holding Alix with his startlingly green eyes.

'What . . . what I mean is . . .' she stammered, 'th—that it was as much my fault as yours, I suppose, and that I really didn't mean what I said at the . . . the end.'

'Ah . . .' Nothing else, just that uninforming sound that emerged so softly it might have been only a sigh.

Alix faltered, then sucked in a deep breath and concluded somewhat lamely, 'Well, anyway, I'm sorry.'

'So there!'

'What? I didn't understand,' she said.

'So there! That's what you meant to finish with, even if you didn't say it.' Quinn's mouth softened into a gentle smile. 'Don't look so defensive, Alix. I'm not trying to start another war.' He smiled again, and nothing in his face or eyes revealed anything but genuine friendliness. 'And if it makes any difference, I'm sorry too,' he said softly. 'Now can we just forget it, and—if you'll pardon the expression— go to the dogs?'

'But . . .'

'But nothing! It's over . . . finished . . . done. Now get yourself organised and be quick about it or I won't buy you any fairy-floss.' He was already pushing away from the table, and Alix had little choice but to follow his example.

Infuriating man, she thought as she gathered handbag and accessories together and dashed to join him at the door. Arrogant, infuriating, and . . .

The hire car took them to the Brisbane Exhibition Grounds and after giving the driver instructions for their collection, Quinn led Alix straight to the dog judging area, arriving just as the first German Shorthaired Pointer class came into the ring.

'Just in time,' he muttered caustically. 'Two seconds later and you'd have been buying your own fairy-floss, young lady.'

'I'm always punctual,' Alix replied lightly, her mood greatly improved by the tangible excitement of the Show, of his apparent acceptance of her apology, and by having somehow been able to push aside the bad feelings created the night before.

'Just one more attribute to set you aside from the common herd,' he quipped, and then turned away to scowl at the judge's initial decision.

During the next two hours they said nothing to each

other of a personal nature, but their conversation centred around the dogs, the judge's decisions and comments, and their shared interest in the breed on show. Quinn seemed to know virtually every one of the exhibitors, and nodded politely to many, but all those involved in the show were too busy with preparations to stop and talk.

Alix revelled in it all. She was here, with Quinn, with their differences forgotten and both of them in a pleasant, relaxed, holiday mood. Sighing deeply, she looked out at the ring and halfheartedly wished she could have entered Nick, because so far none of the dogs in his class appeared quite as good.

'Although I suppose I'm prejudiced,' she admitted half aloud. Quinn turned as if to ask her what she had meant, but was halted by an all-too-familiar voice calling a greeting to him.

Michelle! Alix's insides shrivelled like frying bacon. She should have expected it—indeed *had* expected it in some forgotten corner of her mind—yet nothing could prepare her for the reality.

Michelle patently ignored Alix as she strode over to kiss Quinn lingeringly on the mouth—a kiss, Alix noticed, he made no effort to evade. Only Michelle could wear white to the Brisbane Show, Alix thought. Or at least only Michelle could wear white and somehow manage to keep her casual-expensive white clothing looking totally cool and immaculate.

She was chiding herself for being so catty when Michelle turned, as if seeing her for the first time, and then politely muttered, 'Good day, Alix. I didn't know you were coming for the Show.'

Alix didn't reply aloud, but she nodded a greeting that Michelle pointedly ignored in her haste to reclaim Quinn's attention. With a familiarity that fairly made Alix squirm inside, she took Quinn by the arm as she leaned intoxicatedly and enticingly against him, whispering something into his ear that brought a brief bark of laughter.

Damn the woman! Damn her entirely to hell, Alix thought, wishing she could summon the nerve to simply walk away and leave the two of them to their snuggling and cooing. But she couldn't, of course, not that it helped to realise it.

A hand at her elbow made her start with slight alarm, and she turned to find herself facing the broad smile of Derek Sanderson.

'Well, good morning,' he grinned. 'I rather expected I'd find you here. Come along and I'll buy you something to drink.'

He was already steering her away when Alix halted in her tracks. She couldn't just walk off without a word, disregarding that a moment ago she'd been thinking of doing exactly that. But when she said as much to Derek, he merely shrugged and turned to shout Quinn's name, and when Quinn turned, Derek pointed quickly to both Alix and himself and mimed the action of drinking.

Quinn raised one eyebrow and his mouth quirked into a wry grin, but his eyes locked with Alix's in a fashion that made Derek's presence take on a sudden, almost sinister implication. Then, with a shrug, he waved one hand carelessly as if in agreement and turned his attention once again to Michelle.

And so much for you, Alix thought ruefully. Well, perhaps it was no more than she deserved anyway, and even Derek's company was infinitely better than playing gooseberry to Quinn and Michelle.

If Derek felt himself to be a poor second choice, he gave no indication of it, but instead showed every inclination to pick up where he had left off the night before. Taking Alix by the hand, he shouldered a path through the crowd until he had found a kiosk where they could sit and enjoy a drink without having to stand and fight off the crowds at the same time.

In the harsh light of day, Derek's resemblance to Bruce was less obvious, but daylight did nothing whatsoever to shade his obvious brash immaturity, and within a few minutes Alix was wishing she had simply stayed and watched the dog judging. But when she suggested returning, Derek brushed aside the idea.

'Don't tell me you're as besotted with canines as Quinn is?' he said. 'I mean, I don't mind with him; it made it rather easy to figure out where you'd be. But surely you don't want to spend the day watching a bunch of old stodgies parading their pets?'

'Yes, I do, actually,' Alix replied. 'Or at least I want to see the rest of the G.S.P. judging, because I have one I reckon is at least as good as any I've seen so far.'

He returned her to the judging then, if somewhat without much good grace, only to Alix's dismay he showed no sign at all of making himself scarce afterwards. Or of being quiet—and that was the worst part. She could have put up with his company, but his chatter combined with the heat of the sun to give her a whopping headache.

As luck would have it, they had returned to a point directly across the ring from where Quinn and Michelle were standing, and just as Alix gave a painful little shake of her head at one of Derek's worst jokes and reached up to press upon her eyelids with her fingertips, she looked up to see Quinn staring not at the dogs, but at her. Or was he? It lasted so short an instant that she couldn't be sure. Just when she thought she had actually met his eyes, he looked away again.

And then, to her surprise, he looked back—directly at her and no mistake this time, because he winked! And taking Michelle by the arm, he leaned down to whisper something into her ear before leading her round the outskirts of the crowd on a route that would bring them to where Alix and Derek were standing.

Derek looked expectably impressed when Quinn introduced him to Michelle, but much to Alix's surprise Michelle appeared even more impressed, and she turned on her charm so brightly that Derek became the personification of the classic Australianism—the 'stunned mullet'.

Alix was still trying to sort out what had happened when Quinn took her arm and steered her away, muttering that she'd better get out of the sun. If Derek even noticed her departure she would have been surprised.

They were a hundred metres away, and still shifting easily through the crowd, when Alix looked up to suddenly realise that Quinn was happily chuckling to himself as if enjoying the greatest private joke on earth.

'What have you done?' she asked abruptly, and when his eyes shifted back she repeated it. 'What have you *done?*'

'I told Michelle he was a keen Samoyed fancier,' Quinn chuckled. 'She'll be all over him like a dirty shirt for the rest of the afternoon.'

'You didn't!' Alix couldn't contain her surprise. 'But . . . but he doesn't even *like* dogs.'

'Ahah! You know that and I know that, but do you think he's going to tell *her* that?' And again he chuckled, only this time the mischievous element in his laugh wasn't hidden. It was a side of his nature that Alix had never seen before, and despite her own pleasure at being returned to his company, she was somewhat taken aback.

'But . . . but why?' she asked.

'One way to get rid of the little twit . . . or would you rather share yourself between us?' he asked sarcastically. 'I got the distinct impression young Sanderson was giving you a headache.'

'He was,' Alix replied ruefully. 'But that's nothing to what Michelle will be giving you once she finds out. Or doesn't that bother you?'

Quinn shrugged. 'Not especially.' The unspoken but obvious implication was that he was so sure of Michelle he could risk such a deception, and Alix shivered a little inside. What kind of man would do such a thing to somebody he cared for? she wondered. It didn't seem at all like Quinn . . . and yet . . .

Suddenly the humour of it struck her, and she began to giggle. The giggle matured quickly into full-blown laughter, and even this grew as she heard Quinn's deeper voice join in. She couldn't see him for the tears of laughter that filled her eyes, but as she stumbled, bent almost double by the spasms of laughter, his hand took her arm to steady her.

The rest of their visit to the show was a time of untrammelled delight for Alix. Quinn seemed to have shed all of his seriousness and sobriety in his manipulations of Derek and Michelle, and he became almost boyish in his company. They stuffed themselves on fairy-floss and waffles and assorted other junk, including some especially tantalising candy apples that neither could resist. They went on many of the rides, ventured into side-shows that neither would have bothered with on their own, and toured the various agricultural and commercial exhibits.

'I haven't enjoyed a show so much since I was sixteen,' Alix told Quinn when they finally returned to the hotel in the late afternoon. 'But I must admit I won't be sorry to see the inside of a shower; I feel like I'm carrying half the showground around with me.'

'Well, I don't know what's left for the people, then, because I've got the other half,' he responded with a grin. 'And it's a good thing we have separate rooms or there'd be a war to see who'd have the shower first. You'd lose, by the way, because I'm no gentleman in such matters.' Then he shot a wry look at her and said, 'although on second thoughts I could perhaps be seduced to share . . .'

'No, thank you,' she laughed. 'I'm perfectly capable of scrubbing my own back. I just hope Brisbane isn't having any water shortages, because I think I may be under the shower for quite some time.'

'I can't imagine it being a problem in this hotel,' he said drily. 'Just see that you're ready for a sundowner about six-thirty, and tonight we'll see if we can manage dinner without all the business trimmings. Something nice and quiet and peaceable—and not too late—would suit me very well indeed.'

'Second the motion,' Alix replied. Whereupon she retired to her own room, spent almost half an hour beneath the shower, and then lay back for a much-needed nap. But not before plaiting her hair into a style that would let it dry properly. She had no idea what Quinn might mean by 'nice and quiet and peaceable', but expected it could range anywhere from Chinese takeaway to some hidden little restaurant with superb food and 'quiet' atmosphere.

Secretly she rather hoped for the latter, and was glad she had brought at least one more dress that was remotely suitable for dining out.

She had just entered the lounge room of the suite when the telephone began to ring, and Quinn poked his head through the doorway to his room. 'Answer it, would you please, Alix,' he said. 'I'll just be a minute.'

She picked up the receiver, identified herself, and was hardly surprised when the caller asked for Quinn. She was just turning to call him when Quinn emerged from his room to take the telephone from her, and she was surprised that he appeared to be somewhat annoyed.

His first words, however, showed a change from annoyance to pleasure, and told Alix their quiet evening alone was about to suffer a drastic change.

CHAPTER SEVEN

'Jimmy, you old bushwhacker! I should have known I couldn't sneak in a few days in Brisbane without you finding out,' Quinn said into the telephone.

And then: 'He's here already? Fantastic! Surprised I didn't see you at the show . . .

' . . . Well, of course the trials are still on next weekend; you don't think we'd let Andrew come all this way and then forget about him . . .

' . . . Tonight? Well . . .' He looked across at Alix with an expression that combined super-confident male adult with eager, enthusiastic small boy. ' . . . Yes, fine, mate. About an hour—but we won't stay long; I have other plans and a long drive tomorrow into the bargain. Right! See you then.'

He was about to put down the telephone when a final question must have caught his attention, for he suddenly looked over at Alix once again, this time with a totally male, speculative appraisal before he answered.

'Yes, exceptionally pretty,' he said into the phone. 'But you won't like her, old son; she owns a G.S.P.'

'Is that supposed to be some sort of recommendation?' Alix asked rather acidly. 'I hadn't realised your circle judged girls on the basis of the dogs they choose.'

Quinn's laugh was both loud and genuine. 'Jimmy Grove does,' he said then, 'but don't let it bother you. He's too old for you, has a perfectly marvellous wife that he loves dearly, and he favours Weimeraners over all else.'

'Oh, well then, he's perfectly safe from me,' she replied tartly. 'I could put up with him being old, and maybe even married, but a Weimeraner owner . . . well . . .'

'That's my girl!' Quinn chuckled. 'Just keep your priorities right and you'll go far. Speaking of which, we'd best be off. Jimmy lives way to hell-and-gone over the other side of the city and we'll be all night getting there and back if we don't get going.'

'Would you . . . er . . . rather go alone?' Alix asked then. She felt suddenly uncertain, not at all sure if she would be genuinely welcome.

'Don't be ridiculous,' he almost snapped. 'I promised you dinner and dinner you'll get. Besides, Andrew's a G.S.P. man, so we'll have Jimmy and Sheila outnumbered. And you'll have to meet Andrew soon anyway, as he's judging the trials next weekend—or have you changed your mind about entering?'

'I have not!' Her indignation was so obviously feigned that both of then laughed, then Quinn handed Alix her purse and ushered her through the door.

On the drive through Brisbane's busy streets, using his own Citroën instead of the hire car, Quinn told her that Jimmy Grove was one of his oldest friends and business associates, not least because both of them held a strong interest in gun-dogs and shooting.

Andrew Jamieson, he said, was a semi-retired Perth lawyer who was regarded as one of the country's top trial judges for both utility and retriever trials.

'But don't think you can work any feminine wiles on Andrew next weekend,' he cautioned Alix with a sideways grin. 'If you're going to prove old Nick is anything but a lapdog, you'll have to do it the hard way.'

Alix shot him an angry look, which he missed because his attention had returned to his driving, but restrained herself from saying anything aloud. You just wait, Quinn Tennant, she thought. And for the rest of the journey she consoled herself with thoughts of his surprise when the trials revealed Nick to have a good deal more training than he imagined.

During her solitary walks with the dog since the challenge had first been issued, Alix had concentrated heavily on his training, and she felt Nick was as ready as he would ever be to show Quinn he was anything *but* a lapdog.

'And then won't you be surprised, Mr Know-it-all!' she muttered half aloud, and then giggled silently at the curious look the remark drew from the driver.

When they reached Jimmy Grove's home, Alix

attempted to stay somewhat in the background as the three men greeted each other with warm enthusiasm. But having greeted Quinn, the diminutive, grey-haired man immediately cast an authoritative eye over Alix and said, 'You'll have to marry this one, old mate. My word, you will!' And to the amusement of the other two men and Alix's total mortification, he walked round her, pointing up her qualities as if judging a dog show. 'The only fault I can see is her taste in dogs,' the old man chuckled, 'but in your eyes she ought to be perfect.'

'In my eyes she just might be,' Quinn replied, and Alix looked up, startled, to find him regarding her with a warmth she had never experienced before. It was almost too much, after the older man's ribbing, and Alix found herself locked in a stare in which Quinn's green eyes held her own with a magnetism that sent her weak in the knees and quite lightheaded.

'Personally, I don't know if that's any compliment,' interjected the third man, Andrew Jamieson. 'I'm inclined to think her taste in dogs is far better than her taste in men if she runs around with you, Quinn. A girl this pretty needs a man of distinction, a mature man, not a young pup like you.'

'The way you two old goats carry on, I couldn't imagine a sensible girl wanting either one of you,' came a strange voice from the doorway, and Alix looked up to meet the friendly gaze of a tiny, white-haired woman who smiled warmly and reached out a welcoming hand.

'I'm Sheila Grove,' she said. 'The little noisy one is my husband Jimmy and the tall skinny one is Andrew Jamieson. Come in and meet his wife and we'll have a drink while they go off to look at the doggies. Maybe if we're lucky they'll go to the dogs and stay there, in fact. I'm ashamed of you, Quinn Tennant, not even introducing this child properly before turning those two old lechers loose.'

'Who had a chance?' he replied with a grin, reaching down to plant a loud kiss on the tiny woman's cheek. 'And we'll *all* come in for a drink. I've seen those scrubbers that Jimmy calls gun-dogs and I'm still not impressed.'

The next half-hour was alive with feint and thrust as the

friends argued and quarrelled and sniped at each other
about the respective merits of their chosen dogs, and Alix
found herself drawn into verbal playground with comfortable ease. Ann Jamieson, a tall, lean, yet vital woman,
proved to be as much of a stirrer as any of them, and the
atmosphere was alive with the kind of friendly, comfortable repartee that Alix remembered from her own home
when her parents were still alive.

Only Andrew Jamieson was relatively quiet, apparently
deep in thought for some minutes and oblivious to the gay
raillery surrounding him.

'McLean!' he interjected suddenly, halting a quip from
Jimmy in mid-sentence. 'By heavens . . . you're from Melbourne, aren't you?' And without waiting for a reply, 'I
remember you now . . . you're Doc McLean's daughter . . .
Ho, Quinn, you sure picked a winner this time! Alix's
father was one of the best Labrador men in the country
until he got smart and switched over to raising G.S.P.s.'

Then he laughed out loud at Quinn's slightly surprised
expression. 'And you didn't even know, did you? My very
word you didn't. Hah! Well, I'll tell you something else
you don't know—this girl's father bred both the grandparents of that liver bitch of yours. Alix probably knows
more about her pedigree than you do.'

Quinn joined in the laughter, despite it all being at his
own expense, but several times during the hour that followed Alix caught him looking at her rather suspiciously.

He said nothing, however, and indeed had little chance
to. Andrew Jamieson monopolised Alix entirely after that,
recalling a host of shooting experiences in which he and
her father had taken part over the years. Most of them
were before Alix was born, and she tried valiantly to steer
Andrew away from any tales that might add to Quinn's
suspicions; she didn't want him finding out too much about
her own involvement in such activities until the coming
trials.

Sheila Grove halted the conversation at one point to
invite Quinn and Alix to stay for dinner, and Quinn
accepted after seeking and receiving a nod of approval
from Alix. Shortly after dinner, however, he declared the

need for an early night, and they returned to the hotel not long after ten o'clock.

Alix was somewhat surprised that Quinn said nothing during the drive about her father's dog-breeding activities, especially considering his personal involvement because of Anna. She was quiet during the drive because she had already formulated an answer to any questions he might raise, but it wasn't required.

Instead, once they had reached their suite, Quinn said only that he had quite enjoyed the evening despite the change in plans, and Alix had to agree.

'A nightcap?' he asked then, 'or are you ready to call it a night and head off to bed?'

'Actually, I wouldn't mind a small sherry,' Alix replied, and although she didn't really want the drink, it was all she could think of as an excuse to prolong the evening.

It *had* been pleasant; especially because of the change in plans, Alix thought. The Quinn who had shared his evening with good friends of long standing was yet another Quinn she had never seen, and from many points of view quite the nicest of the facets she had experienced with this multi-sided man.

He was . . . more . . . boyish, somehow, quicker to laugh, to smile, to share himself. The aloofness so necesssry in business was shed like an unneeded cloak, as was the harsh masculinity that both attracted and repelled her. Even now, in the sanctity of the hotel suite which only a day before had been rife with an atmosphere of sexuality and passion, there was now only a glow of comfortable ease, of pleasant, shared experience.

After bringing her sherry, Quinn took his own drink and went to stand at the window, staring down at the passing traffic and the myriad lights of the busy city. At first Alix thought he was upset with her, but after a moment she realised he was only enjoying the quiet and gentle peace of the luxurious room. And he was sharing it, without the need for obvious speech or action.

The whole scene was so . . . domestic, by comparison to the tension-fraught incidents of the night before, that Alix couldn't help the lump which rose to her throat. If Quinn were to think of making love to her tonight, she thought, it wouldn't be with violence and harshness, but with a gentleness that matched the pleasant mood of the evening. But would that make much difference? Deep in her soul she knew it might make *all* the difference. Just the thought of it had a stirring effect upon her.

Even as she sat there, watching him with the certainty that he wasn't aware of her observation, Alix could feel the light tingling somewhere below her tummy, a warm spacious feeling that gradually extended itself upward to the fullness of her breasts and downward to weaken her knees.

She longed to rise and go to him, to tangle her fingers into the shaggy curls of tobacco-coloured hair at his collar, to feel the shifting of the muscles in his back and shoulders, to smell the clean, masculine fragrance of him against her own lighter scent.

In her mind, she felt again the touch of his fingers, his lips upon her breasts, and in her mind she dissolved the anger and tension so that all she remembered was the exquisite delight that had surged through her entire body. So real was the impression that Alix, eyes closed now, sighed softly and shifted her crossed legs—then opened her eyes to find Quinn turned and regarding her with a slightly quizzical expression.

'Are you all right?' he asked, and his voice was a breeze-like caress in the quiet of the room.

'Y-yes,' she replied, suddenly aware of how her movement must have looked to this experienced man, and slightly embarrassed by what she felt.

'I think you're more tired than you realised,' he said softly. 'And you've barely touched your drink.'

'Yes,' Alix agreed hesitantly. 'I . . . thought I wanted it . . .'

'Until you had it—a typical feminine reaction,' he interjected. And as she lifted the glass, 'And don't think you must drink it just because it's been poured.'

He crossed the room swiftly and took the glass from Alix's suddenly nerveless fingers. He replaced it on the sideboard, just out of her reach, then returned to his post by the window and his enigmatic silence.

Both of them were silent for a few minutes, each alone with thoughts that might have been shared but were not. Alix had no idea what Quinn was cogitating about, and she was just as glad that—for once—he seemed to be making no effort to read her mind. He'd have had a shock if he did, she thought with a silent, hidden-inside laugh. Or was he already aware of how much his mere presence could stir her emotions, not to mention her physical responses?

Difficult to imagine, especially considering her near-hysteria of the night before, but Alix couldn't believe that Quinn was totally unaware of his attraction for her. Nor of hers for him, although she was forced to wonder how much of that was purely physical. Was there any possibility that he might one day come to hold the same emotional feelings as she herself?

His inherent gentleness, she believed, made it at least possible, and yet he held a definite and often obvious wariness of all women, as his latest remarks indicated. Could he really be so cynical ... perhaps too cynical?

Eyes closed once again, she revelled in the fantasy of them being together, here in this luxurious suite, but without the reins and bridles of convention to hold back their lovemaking.

Alix considered herself a somewhat old-fashioned girl, at least in her attitude towards sex before marriage. But with Quinn her inhibitions were only intellectual, and she knew increasingly that they were inhibitions that could fall easy prey to the tigerish emotions that seemed far closer to the surface than ever before in her life.

Bruce had never stirred such emotion within her; he had, in truth, never really tried to. And yet she was unsure if Quinn Tennant had ever actually *tried* to stir her emotions, only her physical reactions, and there he succeeded only too well. She smiled to herself at the thought, then jerked away into instant alertness at the touch on her hands.

'Don't get so edgy; I'm not planning to rape you or anything,' said Quinn, leaning down to regain his light-fingered grasp on her fingers and lift her upright.

'You've been falling asleep again,' he said with a slow, gentle grin. 'And this is hardly the place for it. Now off to bed with you, and don't worry about setting an alarm, because there's no real need for a terribly early start. As long as we're back by five or six o'clock, everything will be right, so sleep as long as you need to.'

And before Alix could say a word, he had ushered her to the door of her room, kissed her ever so lightly on the forehead, as if she were a child, and eased her inside. She managed only a whispered goodnight before he had shut the door and left her to a sudden, resentful loneliness.

Slowly undressing, she lay down upon the large bed, eyes now wide with unexpected wakefulness and her entire body tingling with a need that seemed ready to overwhelm her. So real, so tender had been her fantasies of only a few minutes before that Quinn's abrupt ignorance of them seemed almost insulting, and Alix let the resentment build in her mind until it was throttled by logic.

'My God!' she whispered to herself. 'Last night you heaped insults on him for trying to make love to you, and tonight you do the same thing because he didn't try. It isn't much wonder he's cynical about women; with you as an example it's well deserved!'

But logic could do nothing for the languorous tingling of her body beneath the sleek fabric of her nightgown; for the tautening of her breasts and the fluttery feeling in her middle as she lay thinking of Quinn and wishing that she hadn't so insulted him, that he would step through the door that very instant to take her into his arms and give her the physical love that her body craved like a drug.

The sensuousness of her thoughts made sleep difficult and so light that she was wide-eyed at the slightest sound, fearful that he would come – equally fearful that he would not. He didn't, and as the slow hours of the night drifted past Alix slipped slowly into a deep and untroubled sleep that was broken only when her healthy young body decided she'd had enough.

Her wrist-watch told her it was already almost ten o'-clock, and she leapt from bed to shower to travel clothing with surprising efficiency. How could she have slept so late?

She entered the sitting room of the suite with considerable trepidation, only to find that she was apparently alone. The only sign of Quinn was a note propped beside an empty breakfast tray that signified he'd vacated the suite some hours before.

'Hope you don't sleep TOO late,' it said. 'Asked that you not be disturbed before eleven, and we're leaving at noon provided I get back by then.'

It was signed only with a massive, scrawled 'Q' with neither salutation nor closing, and the only personal aspect was the sarcastically capitalised 'TOO'. Not terribly auspicious, Alix thought, but hardly what she must consider ominous.

She rang down for breakfast, just coffee and toast since they would be travelling for some time and she found that she worked best without a heavy meal in her, then hurried to finish her packing before the breakfast arrived. If Quinn arrived back early and she was ready, they might get an earlier than expected start, which should do something to offset her impression of being a layabed.

But he didn't return early, and having exhausted every scrap of reading material in the suite, including the local morning paper, Alix finally took the risk of not being there on Quinn's arrival and slipped away for ten minutes to purchase a couple of magazines.

He still hadn't returned when she got back, but walked in at precisely noon with—of all people—Michelle Keir hard on his heels. The slender, dark-eyed girl gave no evidence of surprise at seeing Alix in the suite, but the venomous look she slipped when Quinn's back was turned told its own story.

Michelle, it seemed, was having car trouble again. She had contacted Quinn quite early in the morning to seek his help in getting some proper action from the service station where her vehicle was now lodged, but even Quinn could do little to effect repairs to a badly abused transmission on a weekend. But he could, of course, offer Michelle a ride back to Bundaberg, and had done so.

Alix was certain at least half the situation was deliberately arranged, but she said nothing, even when Michelle co-opted the front passenger seat and spent the entire journey ensuring that Alix took no part in the conversation and indeed might as well not have been there at all.

Thank heaven I bought the magazine, Alix thought. She could only imagine the horrors of the trip had she been forced to sit in silence, listening to Michelle's chatter as she herself was pointedly ignored.

Not that Quinn was guilty of ignoring her. It was only that Michelle revealed herself as an expert in turning any of his comments around so as to exclude Alix from further involvement in the conversation. What silences occurred Alix made no attempt to upset, since she preferred quiet travel herself and anything, she thought, would be an improvement over Michelle's incessant chatter.

Had she and Quinn been alone on the trip, as expected, there would have been virtually no conversation, she realised, and took some satisfaction from a remembered comment that he, too, preferred to drive without a lot of talk.

Perhaps he, too, was annoyed by the magpie-like chatter, Alix thought. Not that he revealed anything by his manner, but he abruptly refused Michelle's one suggestion that they pause for a snack, saying he must return as early as possible for business reasons. His responses to her kaleidoscope of chatter were brief, but never rude, and although Alix got the impression that he was trying to stifle conversation, he was never really obvious about it.

Alix tried her best to lose herself in her reading, and even at one point considered a nap. The smooth passage of the big Citroën through the gradually lessening traffic was almost hypnotic, especially under Quinn's casual yet expert handling.

It was no surprise when he took the Goodwood road instead of following the main highway into Bundaberg, and less of a surprise when Michelle manipulated things to ensure that he would drop Alix off first and then take her home.

'I have to give you credit, Michelle; you're a dandy manipulator,' Alix muttered under her breath, but although she was slightly hurt by the ease of Michelle's manipulation, it was almost worth the pain just to slide out of the car and know she wouldn't have to hear that voice any more . . . at least for a while.

'Would you mind telling Mrs B. that I won't be long and that everybody's still scheduled to come tonight?' Quinn called as Alix grabbed her suitcase and almost leapt from the car.

She waved her assent and sighed a massive gasp of relief as the car wheeled away, leaving her to trudge silently round the house to a joyous welcome from both dogs and the sanctuary of her cosy little cottage.

Nick wuffle-wuffle-wuffled his greeting, then whined loudly as Alix turned away without releasing him from the kennel, and his cry of anguish was enough to bring similar whines from Anna.

'In a minute . . . in a minute,' she said gruffly. 'Now just be quiet while I drop this gear and have a word with Mrs B., and maybe I'll take you both for a good long walk.'

But when she knocked at the door of the main house, only silence replied. Surprised, Alix knocked harder and then called the housekeeper's name loudly. Surely she was home; Mrs B. hardly ever left the house except to shop, and she wouldn't be doing that at this time, surely.

Alix knocked and called again, but still there was only silence. Silence . . . and . . .

She cocked her head, unsure of what she had heard, but the sound came again, slightly louder this time. She didn't pause to consider her actions then, but thrust open the door and ran into the house, steering instinctively for the kitchen.

Her cry of alarm at the sight of tiny Mrs Babcock, lying sprawled beside an overturned kitchen chair, was echoed by the elderly woman's puny wail.

'My God! What's happened?' Alix cried, dropping to her knees beside the small woman. Mrs Babcock's left leg was badly twisted and she was obviously in pain. At first she could only moan, but when Alix leapt up to soak a dishtowel and sponge at her face, Mrs Babcock finally managed to speak.

'Twisted . . . my leg . . . fell . . . changing . . . light bulb,' she gasped, but then Alix shushed her. The broken bulb in one corner and Mrs Babcock's few words combined well enough without further strained details. Except for one.

'How long have you been lying here?' Alix asked gently, fearing the answer and greatly relieved when she found out the accident had occurred only half an hour before.

'Must have . . . fainted,' Mrs Babcock. 'The pain . . .'

Alix shushed her again, and after telephoning for the ambulance she gave silent thanks to a half-forgotten first aid course that allowed her to determine that it was probably only a severe sprain. Gently she shifted the tiny woman around so as to take the strain from the injured leg, but she decided against further moving her in case there might be other injury.

A glass of water seemed to have greater restorative powers. By the time the ambulance—but not Quinn—had arrived, Mrs Babcock had managed to inform Alix about her interrupted preparations for an 'important' dinner party Quinn had scheduled for that evening.

'Don't you worry about that now; I'll take care of everything,' Alix assured her with a confidence she didn't feel. That confidence ebbed even more quickly when she discovered the menu Mrs Babcock had planned and the amount of work that remained after she had cleaned up the broken glass, replaced the faulty kitchen light bulb, and slipped into her own quarters long enough to find an apron that fitted.

The fact that Quinn still hadn't returned bothered Alix enough that she wasted five minutes invading his study in a futile attempt to find Michelle's telephone number. She then tried the directory, considered checking with directory information, and decided saving the dinner was more important.

'Damn the man anyway,' she muttered. 'If he's that busy playing house—or whatever—he can just wait for his information. And his dinner too!'

Mrs Babcock's preparations for the dinner had been well under way at the time of the accident, and Alix needed little extra time, she estimated, to keep to the timetable. The soup was the only course she deliberately changed, opting for a chilled Sengalese style she could whip up by adding a bit of curry powder to a canned chicken soup.

The enormous fillet of beef was already stuffed with tender oysters and spices, but Alix was far from certain of the timing involved in cooking such a large roast. And did Quinn prefer his roast beef traditionally pink and succulent or typically Australian and roasted to a fare-thee-well? If he got back in time, she'd have to ask, but if not he'd take his chances and like it.

As she was preparing the sautéed potatoes and several vegetable dishes, Alix decided that nobody would bother with a gigantic fillet if they wanted it overcooked, and so another decision was made.

Alix's major problem was the *pita* bread that Mrs Babcock had originally planned to serve hot with the meal. The bread dough had finished its first rising, and now needed to be rolled into balls and left for another twenty minutes, then rolled flat into six-inch rounds and left for a further twenty before being quickly cooked in a super-hot oven. But how flat? How long to cook it? The Israeli style bread was something Alix had never encountered before.

'Ah, well . . . nothing ventured, nothing . . . etcetera, etcetera, etcetera,' she sighed. 'Damn you, Quinn Tennant—at least you could get here in time to go out and find me some bread rolls or something!'

'And why would I want to do that?' came a familiar voice from behind her. Alix turned, suddenly aware of the flour smudged on her nose and the disarray of her hastily coiled hair, to find Quinn looking at her quizzically.

'Because this bread isn't likely to come out right,' she answered, but before she could say any more he interrupted.

'Mrs B. never fails . . .' he started to say, but this time it was Alix who interrupted.

This is a stupid conversation, she was thinking as she nearly shouted at him. 'Mrs Babcock is in hospital, which you'd have known if you'd get home at a decent time!' she raged, and then fairly flew at him in a torrent of words. Quinn stood silent as Alix verbally demolished him and she was barely aware of what she was saying. When she finally ran down he shook his head admiringly.

'I don't envy the man you marry, dear Alix,' he said. 'But I hope he isn't the sensitive type. Now do you suppose you could calm down and start over? I think I have most of it straight, but some parts got a bit lost in the personal attack.'

Calm down! I'll give you *calm down* right between the eyes in a minute, Alix thought. But she didn't say so; instead she took a deep breath, steadied herself inwardly, and related the facts as she knew them.

'Right, that's much better,' he said then, and actually had the audacity to grin. 'And now that you have all the invective out of your system—I hope—I shall tell you that Mrs B. suffered only a severe sprain, is now resting comfortably, and could well be released from hospital to-morrow or the next day. I'm to thank you for her, and also to tell you not to roll the *pita* too thin. About an inch thick or a bit less . . .'

'But . . . but . . .' Alix was wide-eyed with surprise.

'But how do I know all this? Simply because I happened to be in the hospital when the ambulance arrived—and *not* involved in the rather questionable activities you so loudly accused me of,' he grinned. 'I've never seen a woman jump to conclusions the way you do, and while it's often rather interesting, I take no great pleasure in being consistently accused of lechery, debauchery and general all-round womanising. If I was as bad as that, dear Alix, I wouldn't have time for anything else at all. Now, speaking of time, our guests will be here in half an hour, so you'd best nip across and change.'

'Change? I don't understand.'

'Obviously,' he said rather drily. 'Change . . . you know? Put on something fit for company. I'm a fairly liberal person despite all my alleged shortcomings, but I absolutely will *not* have you acting as my hostess in that outfit. And wipe the flour off your nose while you're at it.'

'How dare you . . .'

'My dear child, the kind of man you've accused me of being could dare anything . . . anything at all. And since you show no indication of apologising, at least have the decency to do as you're told.'

'But I can't be your hostess,' she protested.

'And why not, for God's sake? You're filling in for Mrs B., for which I thank you, by the way, and she certainly would have been the hostess. Or do you think I chain her up under the house when company comes?' There was a hard edge of anger in his voice, despite the calmness, and Alix shivered inside at the chill of those deep green eyes.

'You're . . . you're right, and I'm sorry,' she said then. 'And I do apologise for the things I said. It's just that I was so concerned and upset and . . .'

'And . . . jealous, perhaps? No, don't answer that; I'm not sure I could cope with the answer,' he laughed, reaching out suddenly to brush at the flour on Alix's nose. 'I will say you look admirably domesticated, however. Quite becoming, but not with company on the way. Now run along and change and I'll have a drink ready when you get back.'

Thoroughly confused and somewhat demoralised, Alix could only obey, but she made one last bid for normality as she reached the doorway. 'Will you *please* go and find some proper bread, or bread rolls,' she pleaded. 'I've never made that kind of bread in my life, and I'm sure it'll flop.'

'Nonsense!' Quinn shrugged off her plea with a thoroughly autocratic gesture. 'More faith, dear Alix, that's what you need. Besides, there isn't time, so if it fails you'll just have to say that I made it or something.'

Alix hurried through a quick shower, managing somehow to keep her hair dry, and just before the expected guests she was able to return to Quinn's big house in a dress that was suitable if not exotic. Or perhaps it was more exotic than suitable, she thought, catching the assessing glance he trickled down her body like a warm, sensuous shower.

The deep-veed caftan was one she had constructed herself, using a material that flowed in soft jersey from a pale, soft blue around the shoulders to a deeper, brighter hue that merged into a riot of other colours along the hem. The sleeves were a three-quarter-length cut in wide, butterfly scooping that left her forearms free while aiding the flow of the dress around her breasts and middle.

Alix had never yet found a bra sufficiently low-cut to wear with the dress, and under the scrutiny of Quinn's appreciative eye she suddenly wondered if her choice was not a touch too bold.

Quinn was resplendent in a smoking jacket of a velvet material so dark a green it seemed almost black, and the whiteness of his shirt against his tan made him look satanically elegant.

Alix caught a whiff of his after-shave as he reached around her to fasten the apron, but she wasn't prepared for him to whisper into her ear as he did so.

'You be careful of this dress in the kitchen. I wouldn't want anything to happen to it.'

Alix looked up, startled, and found his eyes only inches away. His mouth was even closer, and he leaned down to brush her lips lightly with his own, a touch so delicate and yet so vivid that Alix felt herself flutter inside. For an instant she thought he would kiss her again, but he turned away to reach a glass from the sideboard and hand it to her.

'Thank heaven for unpunctual guests,' he murmured. 'Now get this into you and we'll see about solving this bread problem.'

'But you can't . . . I mean, your clothes . . .'

'You worry too much, and besides, I have no intention of actually doing anything; I'm a far better supervisor.'

'Just what I need,' Alix replied with a shaky grin.

'Exactly what you need,' he replied soberly. 'Because I, at least, have seen this done once or twice. Enough to know you'll stuff the whole thing if you roll them too flat.'

So under Quinn's directions, Alix rolled out the dough and set it for the final rising while the oven heated up and she completed the other preparations for the meal.

Quinn, meanwhile, stayed safely out of range, told her enough about the guests and their business so that she wasn't totally unprepared, and then entertained her with a series of quite ridiculous jokes until the doorbell rang and it was too late to be nervous.

Especially as he insisted they would greet the guests together, and dismissed Alix's objections as quickly as he divested her of her apron. 'Don't fuss,' he said with a broad grin. 'You look absolutely lovely, and if the bread fails, then let them eat cake!'

'We don't have any cake either,' Alix whispered in return, but as Quinn took her arm and escorted her to the hallway, she straightened her shoulders and raised her head almost triumphantly. Let them eat cake indeed! So long as Quinn Tennant thought she looked absolutely lovely, food was of secondary importance.

The guests, with their wives, were both older men, carrying the stamp of business success and personal triumph. Their wives, too, had that inimitable style that bespoke a good education, and a happy and successful marriage.

When Quinn related the story of Mrs Babcock's accident, somewhat over-stressing Alix's part in the rescue, she thought, the reaction of the guests was understandable. But when he continued, saying, 'Alix managed an excellent transition from guest to impromptu hostess,' Alix nearly fell out of her chair.

Well, you lying devil, she thought behind her smile of recovery. You had no intention of inviting me and you know it!

'I did, you know?' he laughed across the room, and Alix looked up with evident surprise, thus defeating her cool cover-up of the effects his last statement had created.

She didn't dare ask what he meant, but even that couldn't save her when Quinn enlightened their guests without bothering to consult her.

'She's sitting there thinking I'm a liar, but I had planned to invite her. It just got sidetracked because of another commitment . . . and the accident, of course,' he said.

The comment drew a polite laugh from their guests, but Alix couldn't let it drop there. 'I'm surprised you left it so late,' she said acidly. 'What made you so certain I wouldn't already be tied up?'

'Because I read your mind, of course,' he chuckled. 'And

I've just proved it, before witnesses, no less.'

'Ah, you're in trouble now, Alix,' said the elder of the two wives. 'When they start reading your mind it's time to either give in and marry them or run like blazes.'

Alix shot a glance at Quinn, saw what she interpreted as a look of uncertainty, and retorted, 'I can't imagine anything worse than being married to a man who can read your mind! I'll run, thanks.'

'Not until we've tested your cooking,' Quinn shot back. 'If it's not up to snuff you won't have to run; I couldn't possibly marry a woman who couldn't cook.'

'You can always *hire* a cook,' Alix retorted, then blushed at the realisation of what she had implied. But if anyone else noticed, they gave no sign of it. Quinn, of course, did, and his response was to rise to his feet and say, 'All right, cook, into the kitchen with you, then. I'll even come and tie your apron strings.'

'You're safe after all, Alix; it's only cupboard love,' said one of the wives, but the other broke in with an opposing view.

'Not so. When they start following you into the kitchen is when things are getting serious. Marriages may have their high spots in the bedroom, but they survive on the kitchen.'

'Ah, the risks I take just to see that my guests don't starve,' Quinn chuckled—and then insisted on checking everyone's drinks before ushering Alix into the kitchen. First he helped her into her apron, and then, surprisingly, wrapped another one around himself.

'This damned bread is virtually a two-man job,' he said with a grin. 'So throw aside your thoughts of marriage and let's concentrate on the job at hand.'

Which they did, working surprisingly well from Alix's viewpoint to ladle the dough on to hot greased cookie sheets and then stand back to watch it puff up like a balloon in the process that created the pocket inside each individual loaf.

'See? I told you it would be all right,' said Quinn at the end. 'And now I shall rejoin our guests and let you get on with it.'

The meal was an unqualified success, apart from Quinn's deliberate teasing of Alix throughout. It was a gentle teasing, but pointed enough to make the older of the two wives comment that Alix had best keep an eye on him.

But the biggest surprise came after the guests had departed. Alix was somewhat taken aback when Quinn insisted upon helping her clean up, revealing himself to be no stranger to the antics of a dishwasher that he declared to be, among other things, 'contrary'.

'Mrs B. keeps it in line with a kick in the slats on occasions,' he revealed with a grin. 'I usually have to give it two kicks, but eventually I get my own way.'

'So I've noticed,' she replied drily, but the reply gained her only another wide smile. Quinn was in far too good a humour to be baited.

The cleaning up complete, he insisted that Alix stay for a nightcap, and she was able to listen on the extension when he telephoned the hospital to ensure that Mrs Babcock was resting comfortably.

Afterwards he very genuinely thanked Alix for her help, with a seriousness far beyond his joking thanks earlier in the evening.

'You're a girl of many talents,' he said after walking her to her own door. 'But you've got me wondering what surprises you might have in store for me next weekend.'

Alix didn't reply except to smile up at him, whereupon he kissed her lightly on the brow and took his leave, pausing only to call back over his shoulder that she'd better not be too surprising, because he still had a few tricks of his own.

CHAPTER EIGHT

Despite everything, Alix slept poorly. Her mind was troubled by a weird combination of thoughts that ranged from the frankly sensual to something far different, mental replays of Quinn helping her bake bread . . . Quinn helping clean up . . . Quinn kicking at the dishwasher.

The sheer domesticity of these aspects of the evening, coupled with the friendly comfort of dinner the evening before that, had a more vivid effect upon Alix than the sensual recollections of Quinn's kisses, his hands upon her. There had been a . . . rightness . . . about their being together, a firm rounding of all Alix's sensitivities. It had been almost as if they were married, and in her search for sleep she realised totally for the first time that marriage—the whole, total package—was all that she could ever allow herself.

All of her fantasies, all of her deep sexual responses to this man were irrelevant without the total commitment she would have to both give and receive in order to survive in any role where Quinn was concerned.

Survive? Could she even survive without him? she wondered. And worse, would there ever really be a choice? Despite his rather altered attitude towards her, Quinn had never shown the slightest interest in a full-time relationship, in a commitment such as Alix dreamed of. Except, of course, to Michelle, who seemed able to command some consistency of response from him.

The mere thought caused Alix to grit her teeth and moan softly in despair, and the sound drew an enquiring snuffle from Nick, who had been making his own contribution to her sleeplessness. After several days of insufficient exercise, the dog was restless, and had spent the earlier part of the night prowling nervously throughout the small cottage.

Alix was no further ahead when sleep finally arrived,

but upon waking in the morning she fixed upon the one decision that made any sense at all to her. She must leave Bundaberg and all contact with Quinn if nothing happened soon to resolve her problem. She simply could not face the thought of him with anyone else, much less the total wrongness of Michelle, but even less could she accept herself in the role that seemed to be shaping up.

She simply could not be only a temporary convenience for this man, slave to her own physical responses and growing love. It would destroy her even more surely than leaving him entirely.

And so she would go, but not today . . . not immediately. She couldn't leave with Mrs Babcock in her present condition. Even after a return to her home the tiny woman couldn't be left totally alone, with no one even within call. But then surely Quinn would arrange something; he was much too committed to his housekeeper to put her at risk.

In fact, Alix thought, it would be wholly in character for him to decide that she herself could be freed to care for the elderly woman; surely if he could free her for those wretched dog classes he could do so for something obviously more important.

Of course! And after last night, with her self-confessed success at having stepped in to help out in the emergency, it should seem the logical solution.

Alix dressed, put Nick into the kennel after a long run that should improve his humour somewhat, she thought, and then drove herself to work in a sunny, buoyant frame of mind. She sailed through her morning's chores, distracted only by the fact that Quinn hadn't even put in an appearance by noon, and then decided she'd skip lunch and visit the housekeeper personally.

She arrived at the hospital, however, to find that Mrs Babcock had already been discharged and returned, presumably, to her home.

Fantastic, thought Alix, but it was a thought that was followed by one considerably less pleasant. Quinn might at least have told her!

She debated briefly if she had time to fly home and ensure that everything was all right, but a check of her wrist-watch told her there wasn't really time. As she drove slowly back to work, something in the back of her mind kept telling her to *make* time, but when she wheeled into the parking lot and found Quinn's automobile arriving just behind her, she forgot about the warning in her haste to greet him and find out the situation.

'She's fine,' he replied. 'It's only a sprain and not so bad a one as they first thought. Apparently it was the shock of the fall that frightened her . . . and the pain, of course. Anyway, she's back home now and resting comfortably, so not to worry.'

'But . . . but . . .' Alix found herself stammering and silently cursed herself for it. 'But . . . surely you can't leave her at home . . . alone . . .'

'Alone? No, of course not,' Quinn replied. 'No . . . Michelle's with her.'

'I . . . see,' said Alix, and then turned away quickly so that he wouldn't see the effect that statement had wrought. It was as if her world had suddenly shattered into a million shreds and for an instant she feared she would break into tears.

Then Quinn was speaking, saying something that Alix didn't—couldn't—hear for the ringing in her ears. She didn't hear it . . . didn't care. All she wanted was to escape before she managed to make a total fool of herself.

'I'm sorry,' she responded in a brittle, almost fragile voice, 'but I must go in now or I'll be late.' And she fled without waiting for his reply.

Inside the building she fled directly to the washroom, where she flung water against her flushed and burning forehead, then stood, trembling and gasping, as she stared at her reflection in the powder room mirror.

'Fool . . . fool . . . fool . . . *fool!*' she cried, shaking her head as the first tears began to slither down her cheeks. Then the flood began, and she slumped forward, hiding her head in her arms until the torrent was spent and she could once again regard her eyes—reddened now—in the privacy of the mirror.

The rest of the afternoon was sheer torture. She tried and tried—and failed and failed—to turn off her mind, to relinquish the thoughts that crept in to stir up her emotions with green-eyed jealousy, frighteningly volatile rage and tears of sheer frustration.

Even logic had a go. How could she allow it all to upset her so much? Why even anticipate that Quinn should have thought of her, rather than Michelle, to be with Mrs Babcock? It wasn't a logical thing to expect, really, since Alix was his employee, being paid to work, not play nursemaid. Michelle, with her apparently substantial independent means, was a much more logical choice, even though Alix knew full well that Mrs Babcock didn't have a great deal of time for the other woman.

Logical. So why did it hurt so much? Gradually, as logic failed, its placed was taken by anger, and in this Alix had somewhat more success.

Anger at Quinn, anger at herself—mostly herself. Anger for allowing her feelings such fantastic free rein, anger at having let him kiss her, having let herself fall in love with him. Oh, she thought, how stupid! How stupid and silly and girlish to leave—luckily—the influence of one selfish man only to slip openly and wide-eyed into the clutches of a worse one.

But she couldn't stay. It was even more imperative now that she get herself away from this place, away from the influence of this man who could sear her soul with a single glance, arouse her traitorous body with one touch of his eyes, his lips, his fingers. She would go—but not until after the coming dog trials.

There, at least, she would have one slim opportunity for revenge, such as it might be. Given just a slip of luck, she might be able to lead Quinn into some totally ridiculous claim, or bet, or *something*! And then make him eat his words without salt!

Alix accomplished little actual work during what remained of her afternoon. Her mind was busy not with engineering drawings but with plots and plans and schemes, most of them patently useless, and of the quick refresher training she must begin immediately with Nick. Less than a week—not much time, but perhaps enough. And she would begin this very evening, following it up with a session each day at dawn and after work. They'd show Quinn Tennant a thing or two . . . she hoped.

Anger rode with her on the journey home, but sped away like a sunburnt mist as she drove into her car port and walked round the corner of the cottage to find Mrs Babcock sitting comfortably in an armchair on the porch.

'What . . . what are you doing?' Alix cried, her first thought one of alarm. The crutches beside the tiny woman and the elastic bandage upon her knee and thigh were evidence enough; Mrs Babcock shouldn't be negotiating stairs at all, much less alone and on crutches.

'Now don't you start,' was the audacious retort. 'I've already run off that Michelle for trying to mollycoddle me, and I'll have none of it from you, either. It's *only* a sprain.'

'Only a sprain? More like only a broken neck if you're not careful,' Alix retorted in a squeak of anger that was only partially feigned. 'Do you mean to tell me you came down those stairs—on crutches—and with nobody here to help?'

'I did. And I'll do it again if I choose,' the little woman replied gallantly. 'And I'll thank you not to badger me about it, young lady. Why don't you go and make us some tea, instead, and then you can tell me all about dinner last night. I've already heard Quinn's story, of course, but I'm far more interested in your impressions.'

'My impressions of what, for goodness' sake? It was a dinner party, that's all. You know what we ate because you prepared it.'

'Not all of it,' was the reply. 'Now will you just stop arguing and go make some tea.'

Faced with a stubbornness she couldn't meet, Alix did as she was told, and ten minutes later the two women were seated at Alix's small table, the tea steeping gently beneath its knitted tea-cosy.

'Now,' said Mrs Babcock, 'I want to know about dinner. Did everything turn out all right? Did you manage with the *pita* bread?'

'Oh yes,' replied Alix. 'Everything came out fine, even the bread. Quinn . . . Mr Tennant helped with that, of course. And he helped . . . clean up afterwards.'

'He *what*?' Mrs Babcock's look of incredulity was startling.

Startled, Alix repeated herself almost word for word, then added the information about Quinn's assault upon the dishwasher and his knowledge of making the bread.

Mrs Babcock's eyes sparkled, but she was obviously holding back an exclamation of some kind, though when Alix pressed her she staunchly retreated into silence.

'But that isn't fair,' Alix cried with a mock pout. 'You can't expect me to tell you everything and then refuse to say a word yourself. What's so unusual . . . or . . . whatever, in what I've told you?'

'Don't badger me, I'm sick,' Mrs Babcock retorted, then smiled warmly at her own weak joke. 'Really, Alix, there isn't anything to tell,' she said then. 'Except, perhaps, that Quinn Tennant wouldn't know one end of a dishwasher from another—and the thought of him kicking *mine* is quite . . . ridiculous.'

'Not nearly as ridiculous as what you're up to, old girl,' came an all-too-familiar voice from the doorway. Both women turned to find the man they had been talking about lounging against the door-frame, his eyes ranging around the room as if he had never seen it before.

'Why aren't you in bed resting?' he demanded of Mrs Babcock with a stern look on his face, then turned upon Alix with an even sterner glance, as if to say, 'and what's your part in this?'

'I'm not tired, obviously,' Mrs B. retorted with a broad grin. 'And stop looking so serious; I'm not some fragile geriatric, you know.'

'No, you're a stubborn, irascible old woman and I worry about you,' he shot back. 'Which doesn't answer my question. And where's Michelle, who's supposed to be keeping an eye on you?'

Mrs Babcock shrugged her slender shoulders. 'At home, I presume. I'm not her keeper—nor is she mine.' The sudden edge to her voice was not lost upon either Quinn or Alix.

'So you sent her away . . . just like that?' Quinn ran his

fingers angrily through his shock of tobacco-coloured hair. 'What am I supposed to do with you, Mrs B.?'

'Nothing! I'm quite capable of looking after myself,' she replied hotly. 'At least it would be better than being under the care of that . . . that woman. She fairly sets my teeth on edge.'

'You've never complained about her before,' Quinn replied, with only a shade of hesitancy in his voice to reveal the surprise he must be feeling.

Alix sat in a stunned silence of her own, unwilling to be a part of this astounding performance and yet unable to escape it.

'You never asked me before,' Mrs Babcock retorted with a toss of her head. 'And I'm not complaining. I simply prefer my own company, that's all.'

'It's not all, dammit!' he replied in what was almost a shout. 'I will not have you left alone under the circumstances, and that's that!'

Alix stared into her tea-cup, unwilling and unable to look up as the silence gathered around them like a shroud. It was insane, she thought. And she wanted to scream, or run, or do something . . . anything . . . to break the tension that filled the entire cottage like unseen, unsmelled smoke.

'Well?' Quinn demanded.

Alix didn't look up, and Mrs Babcock said nothing, but the older woman must have made some unseen gesture, because Quinn's reply to it thundered through the room.

'Alix? Oh, really, Mrs B.! We can't ask Alix to play nursemaid. I mean, last night was one thing and I'm sure she knows how much we both appreciated her stepping in as she did, but . . .'

His voice trailed off then, and Alix almost jumped out of her skin at the tentative nudge of something against her foot.

'Would you consider it, Alix?' His voice was softened, somehow, but it was a second nudge, more definite this time, that spurred Alix to a stumbling, faltering reply.

'I . . . that is . . . well, I wouldn't mind,' she said lamely, her entire body alive with astonishment at what was happening. Surely Quinn must have noticed the kicks Mrs

Babcock was aiming under the table. My God, Alix thought, this is like some comedy farce. I just can't believe it!

'You're sure?'

She had to meet his eyes then, and she shuddered inwardly at the embarrassment her own eyes must reveal. 'Yes, I'm sure,' she said softly, and shivered when his eyes left her.

'Well, I'm not so sure myself,' he retorted, but he was speaking now to Mrs Babcock, almost as if Alix herself didn't exist.

'Alix is a draughtswoman, not a nursemaid; I'm not sure it's really fair to ask her to do this.'

'Well, it's at least as fair as making her take time from work to help with the Fred Bassett school,' Mrs Babcock snapped with an alacrity that took Alix by surprise. 'Or isn't my peace of mind as important . . .?'

'That isn't the point,' Quinn interjected. 'It's just that . . . Oh, well . . . all right. But don't *you* put up with any of this nonsense, Alix,' he snarled, turning once again to meet Alix's glance. 'Just because this old harridan knows she can run my life there's no reason for you to let her try and run yours as well.'

'Alix and I will get along perfectly well,' Mrs Babcock replied before Alix could say a word. 'Now perhaps you'd help me back upstairs, Quinn. I'm feeling just a bit tired; perhaps I have overdone it just a bit.'

Quinn moved quickly to gather up the diminutive woman, leaving Alix to follow behind with the crutches as he carried Mrs Babcock like a child up the steep stairs at the rear of the house and through into her room.

'You silly old possum,' he said affectionately as he deposited her on the bed. 'Never listen to anybody, do you?'

'Not if I can help it,' she replied with a weak smile. 'Now I think I'll just rest a bit, and I know I won't be hungry later, so why don't you take Alix out somewhere for dinner?'

'I'll do no such thing,' Quinn retorted. 'You're not being left alone no matter how sneaky you try and be. I'll send out for Chinese or something, and when you've rested you must have some too.'

'Oh, now look,' Alix protested. 'I'll find something for all of us when it's time. It's no trouble . . .'

'It's too damned much trouble,' Quinn interrupted. 'You've done your share of cooking around here last night and I won't have you cooking tonight as well.' He paused then to stare disconcertingly into her eyes. 'Or don't you like Chinese?'

'Oh, it isn't that,' Alix replied, startled by the directness of the question as much as its unexpectedness.

'Good, then it's settled,' he replied abruptly. 'Now let's get out of here and let Mrs B. get some rest, before she starts accusing *us* of grating on her nerves.' Strong hands at her shoulders manoeuvred Alix through the doorway before she could say another word.

'I imagine you'll want to change before dinner,' he said when they had reached the main floor once again. 'I'm going to take Anna for a run when you get back, and Nick too, if you don't mind. They both need the exercise. I'll pick up the tucker on the way home.'

Alix could do nothing but nod her assent, barely trusting herself to speak. Everything was going too fast, and had suddenly become much, much too confusing for her. She was shocked, surprised and not a little amused at the scheming of Mrs Babcock, but dearly afraid of what would happen when Quinn realised—as he surely must—how he had been manipulated.

'He's going to blame it on me,' she told the housekeeper when Mrs Babcock, remarkably refreshed, called her in not five minutes after Quinn had left with the dogs.

'Blame what on you?' the old lady asked with a look of exaggerated innocence. 'Really, Alix, I think this has all been too much for you; you're starting to imagine things.'

'I certainly am,' Alix replied tartly. 'And I'm not sure I like any of it. It makes me feel terribly . . . devious.'

'Piffle! You hardly know the meaning of the word,' Mrs Babcock replied with a grin. 'You're far too nice, Alix. It puts you at a distinct disadvantage when you're up against people who are *really* devious. When I was your age, and given your looks, I'd have had that snooty Keir woman off down the road with her tail between her legs before she knew what hit her.'

'Well, I'm not like that, though I don't deny I sometimes wish I was,' said Alix. 'And it wouldn't work in the long run anyway, not for me.'

'So you're backing out without even a fight? Humph!' said the housekeeper. 'I wouldn't have taken you for a quitter.'

'I'm not a quitter. But you can hardly back out of something without being in it in the first place,' Alix replied stoutly. 'And all fantasies aside, I've never been in it here. Even you can see that, surely.'

'I can see nothing of the kind,' was the adamant reply. 'There's nothing wrong with my eyes at all.'

'I'm beginning to wonder if there's really anything wrong with your leg, to be quite honest,' Alix replied with a frown. 'You didn't . . . you wouldn't . . .?'

'Of course not! Don't be silly as well as naïve, child. I'm hardly senile enough to go wasting hospital beds just to enhance my little schemes,' Mrs Babcock replied with astonishing candour. 'But I'm glad to see I didn't stay awake half the night for nothing. You are in love with him, aren't you? Even to the point of thinking of leaving us soon.'

Alix gasped at the accuracy of the remark. 'You're . . . you're a witch!' she cried in surprise. 'Or at least a mind-reader.'

'Just a very wise old woman—sometimes,' Mrs Babcock laughed. 'And sometimes just as silly as anybody else, but let's hope this isn't one of the times. Unless, of course, you don't love him enough to put up a decent fight?'

'It isn't a matter of that,' Alix replied sadly. 'I could fight for him if I had him—and I would, make no mistake. But I don't have him. And he's given me no reason to believe I ever might.'

'Piffle! He's made love to you, hasn't he?'

'I . . . I . . . don't quite know what you mean,' Alix replied, hedging round the directness of the question.

'Of course you do. And you've answered the question as well. Ah, don't look so touchy, child,' said Mrs Babcock.

'There's nothing the matter with being a bit ... old-fashioned, if you don't mind the term. Sometimes it has values you wouldn't expect, because a man can get all the sex he wants, these days; it's finding a girl with values that suit him that's difficult.'

Their conversation diverged then into a general one about modern living and the changes from when Mrs Babcock had been young. And with the removal of herself from the focus of the discussion, Alix quite began to enjoy herself.

They were enjoying a good laugh about one of Mrs B.'s youthful love affairs when Quinn returned, loaded to overflowing with plastic containers of Chinese food.

'My goodness! There's enough here to feed an army,' Alix exclaimed when she had laid out the containers and brought bowls and chopsticks from the kitchen on Mrs Babcock's direction.

'What we don't eat I'll have warmed up for my breakfast,' Quinn replied, and at Alix's exclamation of revulsion at such a thought, 'I've eaten worse in my day.'

'Yes, but surely I can ...'

'You can't expect to be making me breakfast,' he interrupted quickly. 'Both you and Mrs B. will lie in as late as you please, and spend the rest of the day being lazy as well. You're playing nursemaid, not substitute housekeeper— and see that you remember it.'

Alix didn't argue, having decided it would be far better to simply organise their lives without consulting Quinn too much at all. Certainly somebody would have to do the housework, and if she herself didn't do it, then Mrs Babcock would be trying to keep ahead of it, game leg and all.

But not only did Quinn not accept her silence as acquiescence, he was also thinking one step ahead of her, as she found by his next remark. 'And just so you don't get any fancy ideas about the housework—either of you—there'll be a casual cleaning lady here first thing in the morning. And she'll be working under my orders, Mrs B., with specific instructions to ignore any attempts by you to get rid of her before she's done the work.'

'Now why would I want to do that?' the housekeeper

replied demurely, but Alix was more direct.

'Well then, you'd better send somebody over with some of my work,' she replied. 'I can't just sit around all day twiddling my thumbs and watching somebody else work.'

Quinn merely laughed. 'Just can't stand to be idle, can you? You should try paying attention, Alix. I didn't mention lunches, which must be prepared . . . or dinners. And after your last performance, I'm rather looking forward to seeing what kind of cook you are in your own right. Maybe if you're good enough I'll move you out of the draughting room and into the kitchen.'

His mocking grin did little to soften the innuendo, but Alix could only glare silently at him for it. She didn't dare say a word in reply.

Indeed, she hardly had a chance in any event; his next remark was quite as astounding as the one before it—and even more provocative.

'You'd also better spend some time on dog training, unless you plan to look a total fool during the trials,' he said soberly. 'That beast of yours is the most undisciplined creature I've ever run across, unless of course he works better for you than he would for me tonight.'

'Well, I should hope he does,' Alix retorted. Then she snapped her mouth closed and quickly changed the subject, lest Quinn trick her into revealing more than she intended before he saw for himself how well Nick could work.

It was difficult to keep avoiding the subject during the leisurely meal, during which it was somehow agreed that Quinn would exercise both dogs each evening, leaving Alix free in the kitchen. It was only after some deliberate manipulation that she managed to keep him from insisting that they train their dogs together each morning at dawn, but she finally won that round by falling back on the excuse that she couldn't concentrate on training with Mrs Babcock alone, and Quinn couldn't very well shake her from that assertion since it was her sole reason for being in the house in the first place.

Nonetheless, Alix made a deliberate point of training the big dog long and hard during the morning hours of the few days remaining to her.

As soon as the housekeeper had arrived, Alix would be away with the dog for long sessions of retrieving practice in one of the many irrigation channels of the district, flinging her kapok-filled training dummy into water, weed and tumbled stream-side vegetation as she encouraged Nick to speed up his retrieving and ignore the temptations of waterfowl and other animals when he was supposed to be working.

Then it was off to a large paddock where she had seen several hares and even the occasional quail. He was superb as a pointer, but she was less confident about his steadiness when the game was flushed, and grew increasingly apprehensive as the Saturday morning utility trial approached.

She knew that Quinn was busy readying Anna for the trials as well, and wished futilely that she had been less adamant about not going with him. Each morning before dawn he would be away in the Range Rover, returning just in time for work, and each evening he spent at least an hour off with both dogs, working them as long as the daylight would hold.

Most frustrating was his refusal, during the final days, to even discuss the dogs' progress. 'They're coming along,' he would say, and then change the subject. Alix could have hit him, on occasion, for the mocking grin that tended to accompany his laconic remark.

Saturday came all too quickly, and with it an astonishing degree of recovery from dear Mrs Babcock, who had decided to attend the trials as an observer.

The diminutive housekeeper brushed aside Quinn's arguments at dinner Friday night as if they were the quibbles of a student, and Alix found it actually amusing the way she seemed able to keep him in line.

'Of course I'm not planning to walk across the paddocks with you,' Mrs B. snapped. 'But I can certainly sit in the shade of the Rover and watch most of the action through binoculars, can't I? And so I shall.'

She wasn't to be swayed by anybody's argument, and dawn Saturday found her ensconced in the rear passenger seat of the Range Rover, complete with binoculars, a huge cooler filled with sundry cold foods and drinks and a selection of books. The two dogs, complete with all the paraphernalia required for their comfort, took up the rear section of the vehicle, and Alix found herself in the passenger seat in front.

It was a motley collection of gun-dog owners that gathered for the pre-trial vetting of dogs, and Alix felt herself almost overdressed for the occasion in clean, close-fitting jeans, a light long-sleeved blouse, sneakers and a kerchief in case she needed something on her head.

Quinn, too, might have been overdressed by comparison, in trim drill trousers, hiking boots and a light shirt. Only the addition of shutgun and broad-brimmed hat brought him within the ranks of his compatriots, most of whom wore ragged, tattered jeans or shorts, rubber boots or sneakers and well-worn dog club T-shirts.

At least half of them looked as if they'd spent a hard night in their cups, and from some of the comments Alix gathered her assessment wasn't far off.

But it was the dogs who took her eye to the exclusion of all else. The utility trial that day was open only to those breeds considered suitable for pointing, flushing and retrieving game. In this case it meant only German Short-haired Pointers and Weimeraners, and G.S.P.s dominated this field of fourteen dogs.

The four Weimeraners, while excellent specimens of their breed, seemed only pale copies of the much more colourful G.S.P.s, most of which were already straining at the leash in their eagerness to begin the day's hunting. Most were solid liver dogs, but one small, muscular bitch was even more brightly marked than Nick, although to Alix's eye she lacked something in overall conformation.

The trial manager was a tall young man with a massive, fiery red beard and a soft Scots accent, and he wasted no time in getting the show under way. The dogs were vetted, competitors given their numbers, and then they were on their way to a paddock selected earlier for the trial.

It was about ten miles from the city, the last few involving a series of tracks and gates and cattle-guard grids until finally they arrived at the chosen location.

Everyone but Mrs Babcock disembarked and gathered outside the final gate, scurrying through a host of last-minute preparations before being called to order.

The first brace of dogs, each wearing a brightly coloured neckband so the judge and gallery could distinguish between them, were sent out ahead of their handlers, and at a suitable distance the rest of the gallery followed. They had not gone a hundred metres when a hare, somehow having escaped the eye of the first two dogs, flushed from squarely beneath Nick's questing nose, and he almost pulled Alix off her feet in his eagerness to give chase.

He pulled, giving a little yelp of excitement. Alix, hauled off balance by the dog, gave an even louder squeal of alarm and would have been flat on her face if Quinn hadn't reached out to steady her.

'Hardly an auspicious beginning,' he remarked quietly, and she flushed with embarrassment.

Hardly auspicious indeed. Suddenly she began to seriously wonder if she hadn't bitten off far more than she could chew, and her every instinct was to withdraw, now, before she made a total fool of herself.

But it was too late, and if Quinn realised that as well as she did, he was at least kind enough not to say so. So they moved on, following as the first brace of dogs worked, and then the second and the third. None of them struck game, or at least none that could be seen from the gallery trailing behind the competitors at a safe and non-distracting distance.

Several of the dogs in the gallery, all of them G.S.P.s, Alix noticed with dismay, carried on an almost constant whining of excitement, causing the manager to rebuke the handlers several times. It was small consolation to realise that neither Nick nor Anna was among the offenders.

Quinn and Anna were in the fourth pair, and Alix's soft 'good luck' was rewarded with a generous smile and a nod as he moved ahead to join the judge and trial manager. Anna had drawn the red neckband, and Alix strained her eyes, moving right to the vanguard of the gallery as her eyes followed that bright red neckband as it flashed from cover to cover, shifting back and forth in a continuous pattern as the dog searched for the scent.

Twice Anna paused as if to point, but each time she turned away then, working a good pattern but never finding either quail or hare. When the brace had completed that portion of the trial, still without pointing a single bird, Alix wasn't sure who was more disappointed, herself or the dogs.

'There's a few birds out there,' Quinn remarked upon his return, 'but it's getting pretty hot already, and the scent isn't travelling well.'

The fifth brace also turned up nothing, and then the sixth was called. Alix's turn. Her apprehension couldn't be disguised, and Quinn alluded to it when he handed her his shotgun and waved her off to take her turn.

No 'good luck' from him. Instead he grinned wryly and muttered, 'Try not to shoot your foot off.'

Alix sneered at him, but as she turned away it was with the realisation that he had just done more for her spirits with the taunt than he could have more conventionally. Thrusting her chin up with determination, she slipped on Nick's white neckband and sent him off with an enthusiastic wave.

Nick worked his twenty-minute stint with a great deal of style, and although he found no game it wasn't through lack of effort. More important, he worked well and close under control, coursing a deliberate pattern as he cast back and forth in front of the shooters and judges. Not so his partner in the trial. It was a young dog, handled by one of the survivors of the previous night's carousing, and whether because of the man's hangover or in spite of it, the dog played up atrociously. Four different times the dogs had to be called in because of the young dog ranging too far afield, happily ignoring his owner's whistle and shouts.

'Oh, you're a good dog, you are,' Alix cooed in praise when they had returned to the gallery as the final pair moved out.

Quinn merely raised an eyebrow, then admitted, 'He worked well, but with that kind of competition he couldn't help but look good.'

The first round ended without a shot being fired, and after a ten-minute break in which the dogs happily swam and cooled off in a handy dam, it was off again on the second round.

If Alix had been apprehensive before, it was irrelevant to the trauma of being drawn in the same brace as Quinn and Anna. 'But what shall I do for a gun?' she asked, mentally kicking herself immediately for asking such a stupid question. There was always a spare gun brought during a trial, and in any event, as Quinn mockingly informed her, any of the lads would gladly lend one to such a pretty competitor.

She could hardly argue, despite the private thought that she looked anything but her best after several hours of tramping through the stubble. Nonetheless, there had been no shortage of volunteers to help her through fences and the like, especially since she was the only female present.

The man whose dog had played up so horrendously during the first session made quite a point of apologising to Alix personally, and would have stayed in close contact with even the slightest encouragement.

In the second run they were the third brace away, working through heavy scrub above a huge dam where black swans and other waterfowl swam in ignorance of the dogs and men and guns. It was as if they knew there was nothing to fear on this day, and as Alix and Quinn stepped forward to take their turn, Alix wished she could go and join the birds in their security.

The two dogs worked well and fairly close, which wasn't all that surprising since they had been trained together every night for a week. What was surprising was how quickly they found birds. After only five minutes, Nick suddenly stiffened into a rigid, definite point, one forepaw upraised and his nose low and outstretched. Anna swung around immediately to back him up, and once both dogs were steady the judge sent Quinn and Alix forward.

Suddenly Alix was absolutely terrified. The unfamiliar shotgun felt like lead in her hands, and she knew it wasn't fitted right for her. She couldn't possibly shoot properly with it.

She glanced across to Quinn, but he was concentrating on his approach as they slipped in quietly behind the dogs. The birds would flush any moment now, and Alix forgot everything but her own concentration. Would Nick hold when they flushed, or bolt after them, thus disgracing both himself and Alix as a handler? Steady ... steady, she thought, moving each foot forward in a slow, deliberate maintenance of her balance and position.

Then the birds were up, soaring in a flurry of feathers that, even expected, caught Alix momentarily by surprise. And everything came to her as it should. She swung up the gun, sliding away the safety as she lifted it, followed the first of the three birds, fired, swung to the next, fired, and had the breathtaking satisfaction of seeing her dog standing steady as a rock when it was all over.

The rest was anticlimax. When the judge ordered it, she sent Nick first after the farthest bird, and when he returned with it, after the nearest.

And when they moved away again, with still more than ten minutes of competition to go, Alix knew—she just knew—that Quinn Tennant would damned well think twice before he dared ever again criticise *her* dog. Or her shooting, she thought triumphantly.

She was striding along, head high and shoulders thrust back in an exhibition of superb, comfortable confidence, when Quinn's hiss brought her suddenly back to reality.

The dogs—no, *her* dog—had struck game again.

It was truly *too* much! Alix halted in her tracks, eyes fixed on the scene as Nick locked himself in the point and Anna, far off to his left, swung up her head and realised what was happening.

Unable to move until ordered to do so by the judge, she stayed silent beside Quinn, her eyes searching through the low cover as Anna threw her head high and pivoted in a huge circle to catch the wind as the bitch came into position.

Nick was a statue, but Anna moved like a dancer, feet lifting high as she skimmed over the scrub in a high-stepping trot that was so beautiful as to be poetic.

She came into proper position to back the point—

honouring, in the language of gun-dog fanciers—and then to Alix's amazement she danced forward still further.

Beside Alix, Quinn hissed his alarm too softly for the dog or the judge to hear, but Alix heard, and felt him stiffen with the awful certainty of what was about to happen.

Anna paused, but not long enough for Quinn to even think of relaxing. Alix could feel his tension as if they had been touching. Two more steps, she paused again, but then she moved quickly and stolidly forward, the determination obvious in her every movement.

Slowly now, like a mincing ghost of a dog, she stepped closer and closer, passing Nick's rigid figure as she stole the point.

'Damn!' Quinn muttered in futile exasperation. Instant disqualification for Anna, and Quinn's disappointment was no greater than what Alix felt.

Quinn's voice when he called in the bitch was harsh with anger, and Anna responded instantly, as if suddenly realising the disgrace of her actions. She came in quickly, but her carriage revealed her knowledge that she'd been a bad, bad dog.

The hare which had started it all bounded away immediately the bitch turned back, and Nick pranced forward a few steps in halfhearted chase before turning at Alix's whistle and prancing back to sit beside her obediently. He knew that he had done nothing seriously wrong, but he was sensitive to the tension surrounding both Alix and Quinn, and he glanced uneasily from one to the other until she'd reached down to stroke his head.

'I am really sorry, Quinn,' Alix said quietly as they moved together from the trial forefront to rejoin the gallery.

'It happens,' he shrugged, reaching down to fondle the questing nose that kept nudging at his fingers as he walked. 'Lord knows why she did it, and he won't tell, but Anna knows she's been bad, don't you old girl? You know very well how bad you've been.'

His reply was a soft, singing whine of assent from the chastened animal.

'Oh, settle down. You'll have plenty of chances to

redeem yourself tomorrow,' Quinn said softly, and Alix silently prayed also for a better day ahead.

She couldn't have dreamed that it would be much, much worse.

CHAPTER NINE

ALIX woke before dawn next morning, wishing she had never so much as heard of gun-dog trials, much less deliberately planned to show up Quinn Tennant for having criticised her dog.

After Anna's disgrace the day before, the remainder of the afternoon had been hardly more than a blur of activity. Other dogs had competed, they had walked several more kilometres in their search for birds and sometimes even been successful, but Alix had hardly paid attention.

All of her interest was in Quinn and the disappointment she knew he must be feeling, even though he didn't show it in any conventional way. It wasn't his manner to complain, or to whine, much less to take out his anger on the dog.

'There are no bad dogs; only bad handlers,' he had said on more than one occasion—usually while instructing at the dog obedience club. And whatever his feelings about the day's failure, he was if anything only more affectionate than usual to his own dog.

And to Nick, who despite his own excellent performance was beaten later in the afternoon when older, more experienced and better trained dogs found game and handled it with stunning expertise.

'You're shaping up to be a damn fine splendid hunter, old Nick,' Quinn had said to the tired animal as Nick and Anna were kennelled upon their return home.

'Yes, and you too, old girl,' he crooned to Anna, giving her an affectionate pat. 'But I'd sure like to know what induced you to play up out there today. I just hope it isn't what I suspect.'

Alix only half heard the comment and it immediately slipped her mind in the welter of preparations for dinner, but once they had all gathered at table it returned, and she asked Quinn about it.

'You don't think she's sick, do you? Oh, I hope not!'

His face held an unusual grimness when he replied. 'Lovesick, maybe. We'll find out in the morning, anyway.'

'I don't understand,' Alix replied without giving his reply much thought. 'Do you mean she played up because of some jealousy factor with Nick . . .?'

'I certainly do not.' The grimness faded as his green eyes twinkled with amusement. 'And for your information, dear Alix, dogs are bothered far less by base emotions like jealousy than people are. And never when they're working. What I'm talking about is physical; I think she's about due to come into season.'

'Oh.' Alix thought for a moment. 'But that would mean she can't compete tomorrow.'

'I doubt if it will happen quite that quickly,' he said drily, 'but it might very well mean she'll have the same dreamy little distractions that all females seem to have on such occasions, which will mean she won't be working at her best. We'll just have to wait and see.'

'I think that was a chauvinistic and . . . and rude thing to say!' retorted Alix, momentarily forgetting her concern for Quinn's chances in the competition. 'And what's more, I think it would serve you right if she did go all . . . soppy!'

'Soppy . . . that's a nice word,' he said without losing his grin. 'Is that what you do when you're in love, Alix—go all . . . soppy?'

'I really wouldn't know, never having experienced such a problem,' she replied pugnaciously.

'Oh, come now. You don't mean you weren't—aren't— in love with the bloke who stole your sketches and ran off to Canada?'

'I certainly was not!' Truth, which was more than could be said for her earlier remark. Was this man blind that he couldn't see her feelings for him? Or did he simply not care?

'Wh—what are you going to do if Anna does come into season . . . about breeding her, I mean?' Alix asked then in a calculated bid to change the subject.

'Well, the first thing I'm going to do is arrange to have that latch changed for one of your special designs,' he said soberly. 'And the second thing may very well be to lock Nick in *his* kennel and put the key in *my* pocket. Because contrary to the thoughts that I'm sure are running through your little mind, Alix, I do not want Nick and Anna doing their thing, to put it delicately.'

'And may I ask why not? I suppose you still think he isn't good enough?'

'Did I say that?' No smile, but his eyes showed the barely-suppressed amusement.

'You did, and you know you did. But I can't imagine how you'd have the nerve to repeat it after what he did today,' Alix shot back, her eyes narrowed in anger.

'He did a splendid job today, and I'd be the last to deny it,' Quinn replied. 'Which has nothing to do with anything at all.'

'Well, by my judgement, they'd be quite complementary,' Alix retorted. 'And what's more, she'd get just as good pups from Nick as from most of those dogs out there today.'

'I'm sure she would, especially since most of them were also bitches,' Quinn replied with a broad grin. 'But that isn't my point, and if you'd stop being so damned defensive about your wretched dog you'd realise that I simply don't want Anna bred at all. Not ... at ... all.'

'Well, even if you did you wouldn't fancy Nick,' Alix replied sullenly, not the least daunted by his emphasis on the not at all.

'To be absolutely fair, he'd be my second choice,' Quinn said. 'There's an American dog in Sydney they call "Hank the Yank" that I'd consider over Nick or any other G.S.P., but that's only personal preference.'

'Huh! And what makes him so special?' Alix asked, giving up nothing of her defensiveness.

For answer, Quinn rose from his chair and stalked out of the room, only to return a moment later with a brochure outlining the credentials of Australia's first American import G.S.P. He slapped the document down in front of Alix almost disdainfully.

'This is probably a waste of time, considering your present state of mind,' he said. 'But look at it anyway; you might learn something. That is a totally different style of dog from your Nick—and note I said different, not necessarily better. A lot of fanciers who've seen this dog don't like him at all, mostly because he's got a different type of head than is common in this country. Personally, I far prefer it, and having seen the dog in the flesh I'm extremely impressed with his temperament as well.'

'There's nothing the matter with Nick's temperament,' Alix replied tautly.

'He whines.'

'All G.S.P.s whine.'

'Not . . . this one. End of discussion,' he said flatly. 'Now what do you say we have some coffee and talk about something else?' There was no hint of amusement in Quinn's expression any more. He was obviously bordering closely upon being extremely angry, and the silence that grew through coffee and dessert did little to relieve the tension.

Mrs Babcock, who had taken no part in the earlier argument, declared her personal need for an early night, and Alix, after seeing her safely off to bed, decided she'd best do the same.

But not without apologising to Quinn, she thought, no matter how distasteful a chore and no matter how much she dreaded the thought.

She knocked at the door of his study rather tentatively, then louder when there was no answer. Puzzled, she eased open the door and peeped in, but the room was empty.

Where could he be? Certainly not in his own bedroom, which she'd passed, door open, on her way downstairs. And after a quick search, she found he wasn't in the house at all.

He's probably with the dogs, she thought, and shivered slightly because that wouldn't make anything easier. Nonetheless, she squared her shoulders resolutely and walked to the rear of the large house with every expectation of finding him.

Her puzzlement increased when she found both kennels empty and Quinn sitting silently at the bottom of the garden, a dog lying peaceably on each side of him. Nick

rose with a wuffle of greeting at Alix's approach, but Anna
stayed silent beside her master, only the wriggling stub of
her tail signifying any form of acknowledgement of Alix's
presence.

Quinn, to her surprise, bounced slightly to his feet and
greeted her with an unexpected smile. 'Sorry I was so
snappy earlier on,' he said. 'I just wasn't in the mood for an
argument.'

'It's I who must apologise,' she replied soberly. 'I'm
afraid I behaved quite abominably, and I'm sorry.'

'Forget it,' he said sincerely. 'Been a long day, that's all.
How did you enjoy it, all things considered?'

'I was . . . sorry about Anna. And naturally very pleased
with old Nick,' Alix replied with one hand moving down to
caress her dog's ears. 'But except for the fact that there
didn't seem to be many birds, I thought it was rather
impressive overall.'

'Hah! The birds were there, make no mistake,' he
laughed. 'The problem was that most of the dogs, until
right near the end, weren't working very well at all. Trials
like that are pretty new here in Queensland, and I'm
afraid the training isn't all it could be in many cases.'

'I see,' Alix replied somewhat lamely, and after that
they both lapsed into a more or less comfortable silence
that lasted several minutes.

'Well, I'm for bed,' Quinn said then, 'and I'd suggest
you get to sleep too, because tomorrow will be a long day
for everybody. Especially you, dogs.'

They walked back together to kennel the dogs, and then
Quinn accompanied Alix the few steps to the door of her
cottage. He took her arm at the doorway and Alix felt
herself tingle with the pleasure of his touch. Then he
reached out to hold her by the shoulders, very lightly, and
she looked up to meet his eyes.

Kiss me, only not on the forehead, please, she said in her
mind, trying at the same time to hold him with her eyes, to
move him closer, bring his lips to hers.

'Alix . . .' His whisper was a caress that stirred her blood,
but her own answer was so soft that she couldn't be sure
he'd heard.

'Yes?' she said again, louder this time. His fingers closed slightly upon her shoulders and she trembled at the touch, feeling her tummy begin to flutter and her legs ache as she strained unconsciously upward to meet his lips.

Those lips descended, ever so slowly, and then to Alix's amazement the line of descent shifted and she felt their cool, almost chilling touch upon her forehead just before he released her.

'Goodnight,' he said softly, and stepped away from her, oblivious somehow of the magnetism she tried so hard to discharge mentally, oblivious to her need, her desire for him to crush her into his arms and kiss her as he had on other occasions.

'Goodnight,' Alix managed to say, brokenly, before she turned and stumbled through the door into the cottage, blinded by agony and anger, wanting to run after him, to hold him, and yet also to throw something at him.

She cried herself to sleep, eventually, and in the process managed to convince herself that it was her own argumentative nature which had somehow turned him cold. Surely no man could be so totally blind, so callously unaware of the love which she knew must literally shine from her eyes.

She wept, but by morning had achieved an icy control of her own, and was determined that never again would Quinn Tennant get close enough to hurt her. Never!

Her foul temper must have communicated itself to Nick, because although he worked well enough in the beginner's class that morning, he was nowhere near at his best. Even so, he was streets ahead of Anna, who performed in the all-age stakes like anything but the well-trained dog she usually was.

Alix, watching with Mrs Babcock from a convenient spot in the shade of some big gum trees beside the placid Kolan River, where the retrieving trials were held, could only gasp at the dog's antics.

'Oh, Quinn will be so disappointed,' she said, barely able to keep her own disappointment from welling up in tears of sympathy.

'Not particularly,' was the astonishing reply. 'Oh, he'll

be disappointed, all right, but I fancy he's got other things on his mind that are far more important right at the moment. You've been fighting again, you two?'

'No, unless you mean that silly argument last night, but we made that up . . . after a fashion.' Alix really didn't want to discuss it, but she also couldn't bear to rebuff the kindly woman.

'It wasn't last night I was thinking of, although he'd no need of ice to keep the beer cold with you around this morning. So if you're not fighting, you're certainly not doing much of anything else, eh?'

Alix admitted as much, though not with any degree of enthusiasm.

'There isn't anything else . . . period,' she said in a mixture of sadness and truculence. 'There can't be—he isn't interested and that's all there is to it.'

'Piffle!' was the expectable remark from Mrs Babcock, who made no secret, at least in Alix's presence, that she thought Alix and Quinn were destined to make a match of it.

If I could only be half so sure—no, a tenth—I'd perhaps be able to cope, Alix thought. But she couldn't, and there was no longer any logic in trying to convince herself of it. Quinn didn't and couldn't care for her, except perhaps as a friend and fellow dog enthusiast. And that, for her, just wasn't enough.

Yet she couldn't hold her heart from going out to him when he returned with Anna, unqualified after only the first round of the all-age competition.

Nor could she help the warmth that flowed through her when instead of showing his frustration and anger to the dog, he caressed Anna instead and told her how pretty she was, and how damned irresponsible and stupid and awful, but in such tones that Anna—who understood only the tone, not the words—wriggled with pleasure, her stumpy tail flickering as she nuzzled against her master's hand.

All too easy to take one's frustrations out on a dog, Alix knew, but how much more truly masculine, more lovable, more human, to uphold the dog's confidence and love by simply praising it and showing it the love it deserved.

During her childhood she had seen all too often the men who defended their dogs in public, yet treated them abominably in private, or what they thought was private, for the slightest misdemeanour. She knew equally that firm discipline, tempered by genuine affection and fairness, was the only way to achieve substantial success as a dog handler, and Quinn carried that maxim to extremes.

'She isn't happy,' was his only remark when he returned to them after having been unqualified in the first round. No anger, no severe chastisement, no grudges. Quinn Tennant loved his dog more than he cared for any of her trophies—or her faults. Just as Alix loved Quinn Tennant . . .

But to less avail, and it was at that moment, seated comfortably beneath a spreading tree on the riverbank as a hefty, broad-headed Labrador Retriever made his straight line, rushing dash to collect the simulated result of his master's blank-cartridge shot, that Alix knew for certain she must begin planning to leave Bundaberg.

And then Quinn was speaking, saying that he thought he'd return both dogs to their home kennel where they could relax in peace and familiar surroundings, and did Alix and Mrs B. want to see the rest of the trials, or return with him to the house?

'We'll stay, both of us,' said Mrs B., and Alix had no chance to interject because he had already collected both dogs and was turned away before she had any opportunity to say that she would like to leave too.

Quinn returned just in time for the final round of the all-age stakes, in which the field had been narrowed down to only four dogs. Surprisingly, only one was a Labrador Retriever; and even more surprising was that the other three were divided into a Weimeraner, a Golden Retriever and a G.S.P.

'The Lab will win,' Quinn informed no one in particular, handing round icy tins of beer as he sat down on the grass beside Alix and Mrs Babcock.

The exercise involved a double retrieve, one bird being 'shot' so as to land in the water after the other, unseen by either dog or handler, was placed in extremely dense weed along the edge of the large pond being used for the exercise.

The first dog out, the Weimeraner, made a poor show of the walk-up to the exercise, which involved going through a barbed-wire fence in the approved fashion, and then failed to find the unseen bird in the dense weed.

The G.S.P., a muscular, liver-coloured bitch owned by a Bundaberg trainer, worked well enough, but at such speed that she kept over-shooting the planted bird, and although she finally managed both retrieves, it wasn't the best exhibition of its type.

Even the owner had to laugh at the antics of the big Golden Retriever, whose slow, dignified approach to the entire exercise seemed more of a performance than any form of competition. Waving his tail like an erect flag, he seemed to float through the whole thing in total disdain of his owner's commands, though he did get the job done in the end.

'Now we'll see how it should be done,' Quinn muttered as the big black Labrador was brought to the starting point. And indeed they did! Despite being obviously under excellent control, the dog flew like an arrow when commanded to make his first retrieve, and he hit the heavy weed growth with the power of a tank. He was back with both birds in less time than the other dogs had taken for the first.

'Pretty hard to beat a Lab at that sort of thing,' Quinn remarked as they drove home after the distribution of awards and the clean-up of the impromptu campsite around which the trials had centred. 'Straight-line retrieving is something they excel at, and damned few G.S.P.s can even come close in major trials.'

Then he grinned. 'But Labs don't point real well, although I've seen the odd one do it, and despite having an almost perfect temperament they're just not my kind of dog.'

Alix, tenderly holding the totally unexpected qualification certificate that Nick had gained from his utility trial the day before, could only nod in agreement. Certainly she wouldn't trade her dog for the best Labrador alive.

She made a point of telling him so as soon as they arrived back at the house, and was mildly surprised when Quinn joined in the praise.

'A little steady work and you'd be as good as any of them, old Nick,' Quinn said in his extra-soft talking-to-dogs voice. 'We'll have to see if we can organise that before the next trials, and then you can really strike a blow for Women's Lib!'

Alix, who'd been thinking almost exactly the same thing herself, glanced up in surprise. The next trials . . . but where would she and Nick be when that time rolled around? Oh, why couldn't Quinn's 'we' include herself as well? The whole thing was becoming too depressing for words.

Fortunately, the exercise of the past two days seemed to have its effect upon all three of them, and after a light dinner at which nobody said very much at all, an early night for all was declared.

Alix had just slipped into her nightgown, letting her hair float down around her shoulders prior to brushing it, when a light tap at the door of her cottage brought Nick to his feet with an alarmingly deep growl.

'Who is it?' she called softly, motioning the dog to silence.

'Depends whom you were expecting,' came the soft reply. 'I make not a bad Romeo, not such a good big bad wolf and a terrible door-to-door salesman, especially for ladies who keep big dogs to guard them.'

'You sound very much like my evil landlord,' Alix replied with a grin that surprised herself. 'Have you come to evict me?'

'Not a chance,' Quinn retorted with a snort. 'I just came to ask a small favour.'

'Oh.' Alix whispered the reply, and he answered without her knowing if he heard her or not.

'Well, are you going to let me in, or do I start huffing and puffing?' he asked lightly.

'Don't tempt me,' Alix replied just as lightly. She was suddenly beginning to enjoy herself, all thoughts of depression fading with the sound of his voice. 'Or maybe you should try the Romeo bit; I've always fancied being sere-naded by moonlight.'

'Whatever turns you on,' was the astonishing reply, 'but only after you've given me the proper opening. I guess we'll have to dispense with the balcony, though, unless we shift Mrs B. out of her bedroom.'

The quiet chuckle that followed revealed that Quinn was also enjoying the rather ludicrous dialogue. Alix opened her mouth to begin the famous wherefore-art-thou lines, then closed it abruptly. The words simply wouldn't come. Instead she was struck with a horrible sadness that descended upon the frivolity like a shroud. Tears sprang to her eyes and she realised that she didn't dare open the door. It took all of her strength just to speak through it.

'I'm . . . sorry, but it's a bit late for games tonight. What is it that you wanted?'

Her answer was silence, at first. A silence that seemed to reach through the closed door in an icy fog, surrounding her. 'All right,' Quinn said then, very coldly. 'I just wanted to ask if you'd mind staying on with Mrs B. this coming week. I know she maintains she's all right, but she's not so young any more, and she pushes herself. Would you, Alix? I'm honestly concerned at leaving her alone until she's totally done with those crutches.'

'Yes. Yes, of course I will, if you think it's best,' Alix replied, forcing herself to speak as naturally as she could past the enormous lump in her throat.

'Good,' he said. 'I'm flying to Melbourne in the morn-ing and I'll be there most of the week. Having you here with her takes a great load off my mind.'

He paused then, only briefly, but long enough that Alix could almost feel his mind working. And then, 'Thanks again, Alix. Goodnight.'

When she was sure he'd gone, Alix retreated into her bathroom, staring into the mirror through tear-reddened, haunted eyes. What was the matter with her? How could she possibly have changed from a relatively normal, level-emotioned young woman into this . . . this creature whose emotions leaped like . . . like a demented frog from hap-piness to sorrow without any logic?

She must leave, but obviously she could not until Mrs Babcock was totally recovered. How long? A week? Two? Maybe a month at most before she could, with a clear conscience, give in her notice and take her tattered emotions somewhere less vulnerable.

Quinn left on the early morning plane. Or so Alix was told. She didn't see him go, didn't dare to face him after looking at herself in the mirror once her sleepless, tension-fraught night was over. Instead she went off with Nick even before dawn, deliberately staying until she knew the morning flights had gone.

He was gone all that working week, a week in which Alix might as well have gone to work herself. Mrs Babcock gradually assumed control of the household, relinquishing the crutches without any sign of a problem, the cleaning lady came and went without incident, and Alix grew increasingly bored as the days passed.

It was little consolation being able to spend almost as much time as she liked with the dogs. Anna, by Wednesday, began to show distinct signs that Quinn's prognosis had been correct. Was the man always right? Despite knowing there was still some time before actual mating would be likely, Alix immediately instigated a programme of keeping the dogs isolated from each other, even moving Nick so that there was an empty kennel between them.

She worked Nick regularly, morning and evening, and twice a day too, she took Anna into the back of the station sedan and drove her to an isolated paddock for exercise, thus avoiding the problem of stray dogs gathering round the house.

A telephone call brought one of the workmen from the plant to cut off the old latches from the kennel gates and install new ones of Alix's design. That ought to please Quinn Tennant almost as much as being right, she thought acidly, but she did not go to the trouble of fixing padlocks to the new latches.

If he wanted to go to that much trouble, he could damned well do it himself, Alix thought angrily.

She was, in all honesty to herself, both mildly surprised and enormously pleased when he did no such thing, but instead complimented her for being so careful.

He then took both her and Mrs Babcock out to dinner at the Rowers' Club and spent the evening regaling them with tales of what must have been the strangest business trip in history.

'Everything I touched seemed to go wrong,' he said with a wry grin. 'I missed taxis, was late for appointments, damned near missed the plane coming home . . . the entire trip was just one enormous stuff-up.'

Perhaps, but the way he told it, Alix thought the trip must also have been a hilarious adventure in blunderland, and both she and Mrs Babcock laughed until their ribs ached at the stories he related.

His sense of humour was pleasant, considerate, often rather absurd, but infinitely warm. Unlike his every other attitude during the next few days, when he managed without any specific, overt action to give Alix a feeling of incredible coolness towards her.

There was never anything she could put a finger on, just a definite atmosphere of . . . distance. Quinn was never alone with her, never touched her, yet often seemed to be watching her. His conversation was never pointed, ever provocative, but always polite and friendly—yet cool.

And when he announced on Wednesday morning that he was off on another long journey, this time to North America, Alix was almost glad to see him go. At least, she thought, it would give her some time to get her own head together.

'I'm hoping to be back by Sunday, but even if I don't make it I'd like you to consider yourself on overtime through the weekend,' he said. 'By my reckoning, the few days from Sunday onward will be the most . . . crucial . . . for Anna, and if I can't get back for some reason I want to be sure she's with someone I can trust to take extra-special care.'

Alix found herself tongue-tied by the compliment, and could only stare at him, struggling to get the words out as she stammered her thanks.

'Don't be silly,' he said. 'You've done an excellent job of coping so far and I have total confidence you can manage without me.' Then he grinned engagingly and Alix caught a glimpse of the more normal Quinn Tennant.

'Of course you'll have to forestall any big plans you might have had for Nick, but if he's a good dog maybe we can make it up to him next time.'

'Oh, I'm sure he'll be thrilled to death,' Alix replied with acid in her voice. What was this man playing at? She was beginning to think that Quinn's mental state must be as flustered as her own, from the way he switched from cold to friendly and back again.

At that moment it seemed like a quite ridiculous thing for him to have said, especially since he had already voiced his preferences involving a mate for Anna. But it was nowhere near as strange as what he said as he left the airport gateway to catch his plane to Brisbane and onward to America.

CHAPTER TEN

ALIX couldn't believe her ears. 'What did you say?' she asked in total bewilderment, her eyes meeting his in a look that combined confusion with . . . almost fear.

'I asked if I should give your love to Bruce if I see him.' Quinn's voice was unusually low, and there was none of the mocking light she would have expected in his eyes following such an idiotic remark.

'Are you quite mad?' she asked, and then, without waiting for a reply, 'You must be! In fact, I think you should be going to a doctor, not running off to America. You're sick!'

She turned away then, but instantly swung round again to face him as frustration and anger boiled up in her heart, then boiled over in a torrent of pain and hurt and . . . words.

'Yes, damn it. Give my . . . love to Bruce if you see him. Tell him thank you for running out on me . . . because it was the nicest thing he could ever possibly have done for me. Tell him that I never really loved him, any more than he ever loved me. And tell him while you're at it that most of the time I don't even remember his name, except when *you* keep bringing it up all the time.

'Tell him any damned thing you like, Quinn Tennant, because he's obviously a helluva lot more important to you than he is to me!'

And then, with an almost animal cry of pain, she turned and ran, plunging through the airport terminal, forcing her way through startled departure passengers, past the equally surprised rental car girls, down the footpath and into her own vehicle.

Stabbing at the accelerator, she flicked the key, felt the engine fire into life. Blindly, ignorant of what might be behind her and not caring in the least, Alix shot backward, screeched to a halt, then spun out of the airport parking lot in a crescendo of squealing tyres and exhaust smoke.

Dimly able to see the narrow road ahead, she raced out of the airport grounds at a fearful speed, swung hard left when she hit the highway, and then roared away from the city at top speed, her eyes locked on the swiftly-passing bitumen beneath her wheels.

She didn't think, didn't feel, didn't care. And not until several kilometres had passed did she gradually let the vehicle slow itself as reality returned to her. Still, she was only partially lucid when the turn-off to Bingera Weir came into view, and she swung the car to the right and down the rutted, rough gravel track to where a narrow weir crossed the Burnett River as a shortcut route for cane trucks en route to the Bingera Mill.

Parked on the verge, where she could see the wide, slow waters of the drought-shrunken river, she sat and stared into space as reality reassembled itself in her mind. Her tears were past, leaving only an incredible emptiness.

An hour passed unseen, then another. And finally, Alix shook her head like a swimmer emerging from beneath the water, took an enormous breath that seemed to stab knives through her ribs, and started her vehicle once again. She drove back into the city at a speed far more sensible than her exit speed, but she didn't so much as glance at the airport on her right as she passed it.

Back at the office, she said nothing to anyone to explain why it should take two and a half hours to deliver somebody to the airport ten minutes away. She said nothing at all to anyone, not even a conventional greeting as she strode into the building and into the small studio where she worked.

Sitting down squarely at her draughting table, she pulled the most current piece of work in front of her, picked up her implements and began to work. By leaving time that evening, still in silence, she had accomplished an astounding amount of work and had returned herself to normal—for whatever that was worth.

The following few days were spent in an almost absent-minded dedication to the duties she faced. She slept each night like the proverbial log, undreaming, uncaring. She rose at dawn and walked the dogs, individually, before breakfast. She put in a full day's work, but spoke only when she was forced to, and then as little as possible.

Every evening she had dinner with Mrs Babcock, and usually it was in almost total silence, or, at most, in discussion of such total trivia that it placed no mental or emotional strain on either of them.

Alix could only be thankful that the older woman had the good sense and kindness not to try and interfere. In the long run, it made things much easier, and by Saturday she felt almost able to face Quinn again when he returned. By Sunday she was—in her mind—totally ready, only he didn't return.

Inside, Alix was like a gigantic iceberg, although her exterior had by this time returned to something approaching her usual self. She could talk to people now, and be polite—even interested. Conversation was easy, if perhaps a bit brittle.

And especially when she accidentally ran into Michelle Keir while downtown shopping at noon on Monday. Alix was really proud of herself for the way she carried on a cool, easy, light conversation that revealed nothing of the frigid chill inside her.

. . . No, she hadn't heard from Quinn. No, she didn't know when he'd return. Today . . . tomorrow . . . the next day. Yes, the dogs were fine. Anna was at her most susceptible, but that should be over in a day or two, thank goodness. No, Quinn didn't intend breeding her, at least not this time. He's got some American dog in mind, but again, not this time. Dead against it, for whatever reason . . .

She accepted the sultry, preening explanation without a tremor; it fell into the icy depths inside her and disappeared without a trace.

'Well, don't let on I told you, because I think it's still all a great secret, but Quinn has some very big plans for a couple of months from now . . . very big and rather—emotional, I suppose you'd say. Puppies would only complicate them.'

Michelle's own words. Translation: I've finally got him

trapped, so eat your heart out, Alix McLean.

What heart? Alix heard the words, made the translation in her mind, and waved a casual farewell as they separated. You've got him, Michelle, and welcome to him. The emptiness inside her absorbed the message and digested it without effect.

She was readying herself to leave work that evening when the switchboard called through with the message. Would she please arrange to pick up Mr Tennant at the airport after work? His plane was due at five-fifteen. She would.

And she did, only to find the airport strangely deserted upon her arrival, hardly a car in the parking lot. Still, not hers to reason why, or to question. She would wait. And after half an hour she was still waiting. Puzzled, Alix finally got out of her vehicle and strode into the silent terminal building, where a lone reservations clerk shook his head in puzzlement at her question.

'You must have got the timing wrong, love. No planes until almost seven.'

That would be typical, Alix thought, and after debating a moment whether to bother going home for tea, she decided instead it wasn't worth the effort. 'I'll just nip up and grab a hamburger at MacDonalds,' she told Mrs Babcock on the telephone a moment later.

'Whatever you think is best, Alix. It's just that . . .'

'Just that what? Oh, you haven't got something special planned for dinner?'

'Oh, no, dear, nothing like that. It's just that . . . well, he usually lets *me* know when he's due back from a trip. And he hasn't, although of course if he spoke to you . . .'

'Well, he left a message. I didn't speak to him personally,' Alix replied, worried now by the concern in the housekeeper's voice. 'Are you thinking somebody might be playing silly little games or something?'

'Oh, goodness, no. I mean, there wouldn't be any sense to that, would there? No, I'm probably just an old fuss-budget, that's all.'

'You didn't fall again—and hit your head this time?' Alix asked in a bid to infuse some lightness into the discussion and perhaps lessen Mrs Babcock's concern.

'No . . . no, dear, of course not. But I am feeling a bit tired, so perhaps I'll have a nap until you get back. About seven-thirty, I expect?'

'With him or without him, but hungry either way,' Alix replied lightly. 'So don't forget to put tea on before you lie down.'

She arrived just before seven-thirty—without Quinn Tennant. He had been on neither of the final flights for that evening, had sent no message, nothing. Alix drove home vastly confused about it all, but not especially worried.

She wheeled into her carport and slipped from the car, bag in hand. She'd just drop the purse into the cottage, speak to the dogs on the way by, and then go up to Mrs B., she thought.

Inside the cottage, she paused only long enough to unpin her hair, slip out of her office gear and into a casual pair of slacks and a shirt, then she walked towards the kennel block, whistling a soft greeting to the dogs.

Her eyes, gradually regaining her night vision as she walked, widened in suspicion at the unusual silence from Nick's isolated kennel, and then in horror at the snuffling sounds of greeting from Anna's.

Alix ran to the wire gates, unable to credit what her eyes revealed. It was impossible! It simply could not be—but it was. The two dogs were together in Anna's kennel.

Together! And the movements created by Alix's loud shriek of alarm revealed the awesome truth. For a moment she stood in silence, closing her eyes and opening them again as if that action could somehow make the tableau disappear.

Water. A bucket of water . . . but even as her mind stirred in a bid for action, any kind of action, another part of it shrugged aside everything in an empty, almost nauseous reality. It was too late. Purely and simply too late. But she couldn't just . . . ignore it.

'Nick! Damn you Nick, stop it! Stop . . . stop . . . stop . . .!' she shrieked, lunging at the wire and clawing, smashing at it with her hands.

'Leave it.' The voice came from behind her shoulder like the crack of doom and she turned to face Quinn Tennant. His eyes were like flaming green coals as he looked from her to the dogs and back again. Anger had made him rigid as a statue.

Alix recoiled at the sight of him, something inside her trembling at the rage that seemed to emanate from him like an aura, white-hot and livid. His tie was pulled open below the unbuttoned throat of his shirt, one hand still held his briefcase, but it was half raised, almost like a weapon.

And his eyes were hatred itself, a hatred that flamed and curdled with hidden, raging fires that seemed to sear her to the very soul.

'Just . . . leave it,' he said coldly through clenched teeth, then he turned on his heel and strode away, moving like a man going into battle, each step a menacing movement of its own.

Alix stood as if rooted, unable to think, unable to move. Her fault . . . it was all her fault. He would blame her, certainly. Blame? He would hate her, despise her.

'But it isn't my fault,' she whispered. 'It isn't . . . oh, it isn't!' How could it be? She had faithfully kept the dogs apart. They had been apart when she left that morning. Mrs Babcock must have . . . but she *wouldn't*!

'And I didn't,' she whispered, and then louder, 'It isn't my fault. I didn't . . . I didn't . . . It . . . isn't . . . my . . . fault!'

And she was running, across the lawn and up the stairs to the rear of the house. She would tell him, and he would— he *must*—believe her. He must!

Alix reached the back door, breath coming from her in hoarse, gulping gasps. But even as she put her hand on the latch she heard his voice, coarse with anger, and paused.

'. . . bloody interfering bitch. Bitch! I would never . . . never have believed she could do such a thing. How could anyone do such a thing? She will never set foot in this house . . . on this property again . . . or I'll personally wring her neck!'

Alix stood transfixed, wanting to run, wanting to go into the house and throw herself upon his mercy, wanting to . . . to die. And his voice continued, out of sight but boring into her brain . . . into her soul.

'. . . capable of such a breach of trust. Oh, God! How could I be so damned blind? That bitch! That . . .'

Alix heard no more. She turned and fled back down the stairs, leaping down them two at a time, heedless of the risk and ignoring it. Compared to the risk of staying, it was nothing. Into her cottage she ran, slipping on the lights as she plunged through the door.

She must get away. Now! She couldn't stay, daren't stay. Rushing around the rooms like a demented animal, she flung clothing haphazardly into suitcases, bundled dirty clothing and clean alike, thrust cosmetics into their case without a thought of whether they might be open or closed.

A tube of lipstick lost its cover on the way in; she ignored it, as she did the bottle of nail polish that somehow came open and spilled all over everything else.

Get out. Get out! The words roared through her mind over and over and over. One suitcase was filled, then the other. Her jewel box, her cosmetics case. She rushed out of the cottage, flung everything into the back seat of the vehicle, turned back for more.

Emerging the second time, she rounded the corner and floundered straight into . . . him. She didn't need her eyes to know it, her every sense, her every inner feeling told her. The scent of him, the touch of strong hands that clasped her shoulders before she could fall, the voice that was overridden by her terrified scream.

'My God, Alix, what are you *doing*? Alix!' She was held immobile, unable to flee, unable to run, unable to . . . what? The strength drained from her; the bundles fell limp from her nerveless fingers. Her entire body slumped in the weariness of total . . . nothing.

'Alix. Alix! What is it, my love? What's wrong?'

The words filtered into her mind, but they made no sense, had no real impact. Then strong hands had plucked up up, cradling her as if she were a child, and the scent of his after-shave strengthened as he snuggled her close to him.

There was movement, like being astride a huge, powerful horse that cantered easily up, up, up.

'Brandy. Get brandy, Mrs B. Oh, hell . . . Alix! Alix, come out of it . . . oh, God, Alix!' The voice was louder now, stronger and somehow . . . compelling.

Alix tried to open her eyes, failed at first. Then there was a light, tentative touch at her lips and she opened them to feel the sudden sharp bite as brandy rasped into her throat. She gasped aloud, felt the warmth as some of it spilled down the front of her.

The shock of it forced her eyes open, and she shut them just as quickly. There, only inches away . . . him! Whimpering, she tried to writhe away, but arms like iron bars held her captive.

'Alix! What's wrong, love? Mrs B., call the doctor, immediately. My God, what's wrong with her?'

'N . . . oooo.' The word escaped in an ululating croon, then she repeated it, somehow. 'Nooo!'

She was drowning, being pulled down into a blackness that loomed awesomely below her. And then fingers, light, searching fingers like spider webs played across her face, her throat. 'Alix, my love, please . . .'

She managed to open her eyes, seeing before her two green orbs that slowly swam into focus. Eyes. And a nose, a mouth, a face that she barely recognised for the lines of strain, the softness, the compassion that seemed to float out from those eyes and into her own.

'Not . . . not . . . my . . . fault,' she whispered, shaking her head weakly, fearfully. 'Not . . . my fault.'

'What are you saying? Oh, Alix, my love! What's happened? What are you talking about?' His voice seemed to sear into her soul, but the burning was not painful, but somehow comforting, soothing.

'Dogs,' she whispered. 'The . . . the dogs . . . Anna . . .'

'Dogs? What the hell?' For an instant there was again that furnace blaze of anger, but it flared and died almost at once.

'Alix . . . my God, love. Surely you can't have thought

that I blamed . . . oh lord, of course you did. Oh, Alix, what have I done to you? Of course it wasn't your fault; I never thought it could be. Alix, I love you . . . I couldn't ever have believed . . .'

'L—love. I . . . love you . . . too,' she whispered, something deep within her forcing out the words. She was hardly aware of having spoken.

And then those gossamer fingers were on her cheek again, trailing down to caress the muscles of her throat. She felt his lips as they descended to touch her own, ever so lightly, and the taste of him, the feel of his mouth, his fingers, did what his voice had been unable to manage.

Inside her, something had exploded, forcing out the lassitude, the emptiness, the fear. Her fingers moved, her arms lifted to wrap around his neck as her lips parted to accept him.

'I love you.' The words, his words, floated in her brain, repeating themselves over and over as they drove off her fears, seeped throughout her very being, demanding that she accept them.

His lips caressed her mouth, her face, her throat, kissing away the saltiness of her tears, the hot spill of the brandy.

And her own lips responded as her arms locked around his neck, holding him against her, locking his body against hers, his mouth against hers.

It seemed a long time, so very, very long, before both of them floated back to some semblance of reality, away from the nightmare turned to dream of perfection.

She was sitting, no longer cradled in his arms but held close by an arm firm around her shoulders. A glass of brandy, cradled in her hand, could be lifted to tip its warm fires into her, though she was warm enough.

'Michelle,' said Alix, still unbelieving. 'And she . . . knew, when I saw her at noon.'

'Too damn right she did, the bitch!' Quinn's voice was stronger, now that he no longer had to hide his anger. 'My fault, naturally. I'd arranged to do some business for her in Brisbane, and when I talked to her this morning I told her I'd be home some time tonight because you'd already done too much in caring for Anna. I even told her *why* I didn't want Anna bred, because I was planning a honeymoon and I damned well didn't fancy having half a dozen puppies for company. My God! I still can't imagine anybody being so vindictive. She knew there was nothing . . . relevant between me and her. There hasn't been anything between us since you got here, and certainly there never *was* any . . . understanding.'

Unable to contain his anger, he rose from the sofa and strode around the room, pacing like a caged animal.

'If you don't settle down I'll be calling the doctor again and telling him to come after all—for you!' Mrs Babcock snarled, shouldering her way into the room with a tea-tray in her hands.

'Personally I've got very little sympathy for either of you. None of this would have happened if both of you had listened to me in the first place. And as for your honeymoon—well, I've cared for puppies before in my life, and I suppose once again won't be too difficult. Or you can still . . .'

'No!' they both said together. The housekeeper gave them a scathing, I-told-you-so glare and shook her head wisely.

They drank the tea in silence, a warm, companionable silence shared by Mrs Babcock, now that she'd had her say.

And Quinn suddenly grinned, a glowing, boyish grin of pure deviltry. 'Damn, I almost forgot,' he muttered, and rushed from the room, only to return a moment later to hand the startled Alix a heavy manila envelope.

'Present!' he said. 'I was going to save it for a wedding gift, but perhaps now is a better time.'

Puzzled, she slid open the envelope and turned it up so that the contents spilled out into her lap.

It took a moment for comprehension to filter through. 'My drawings! But how . . . you *did* see Bruce. You . . . but . . . what did you *do*?'

Quinn shrugged modestly. 'Just brought certain . . . pressures to bear,' he said. 'I have some fairly powerful contacts overseas.'

'Unbelievable, absolutely unreal,' Alix whispered, and then stacked the drawings into a neat pile which she ripped in half, then in quarters, before anyone else could move.

'Oh, Quinn, I do thank you,' she whispered almost shyly. 'But these are from the past; they don't matter now.'

'Well, I suppose it's the thought that counts,' he replied with a rueful grin. 'Speaking of which, I've just thought up the ideal revenge for our bitchy little friend—something that might even make it up to Anna for *her* name.'

'I don't understand,' said Alix.

He grinned mischievously. 'Anna's proper kennel name is Holzer's Irmgard Anna Carina,' he said. 'The bloke I got her from said he named her after his first wife. Well, what better than to name one of the female pups from this litter after the world's foremost bitch?'

'No!' Alix's tone and eyes made it adamant.

'Well, why not? It would go down a treat at obedience classes later on.'

'No! I would not—repeat . . . *not* . . . do such a thing to any puppy. And especially not to a G.S.P. If you insist on naming anything after Michelle, go out and buy yourself a mongrel, preferably one with Samoyed blood.'

'Whatever you say, my love,' Quinn replied. And as Mrs Babcock discreetly left the room, he sealed the bargain with a kiss that left no doubt at all of his sincerity.

The Mills & Boon Rose is the Rose of Romance

Every month there are ten new titles to choose from — ten new stories about people falling in love, people you want to read about, people in exciting, far-away places. Choose Mills & Boon. It's your way of relaxing:

June's titles are:

RAIN OF DIAMONDS *by Anne Weale*
Francesca idolised Caspar Barrington. But she *was* very young and he did not encourage her feelings for him. Was he right or was she?

THE LOVING SLAVE *by Margaret Pargeter*
Quentin Hurst was at last beginning to return Gina's interest. But could she compete with the elegant Blanche Edgar?

THE EVERYWHERE MAN *by Victoria Gordon*
The domineering Quinn Tennant was everywhere! Everywhere but the one place Alix quickly came to want him: in her heart.

MADRONA ISLAND *by Elizabeth Graham*
Kelsey Roberts had destroyed Lee's life. Now they had met again, but how could she extract revenge from a man who didn't even remember her existence?

SAFARI ENCOUNTER *by Rosemary Carter*
Jenny had to let the forceful Joshua Adams take over her father's game park. But her real problems began when Joshua took over her heart as well . . .

WHERE TWO WAYS MEET *by Yvonne Whittal*
The social gap between Margot Huntley and Jordan Merrick was too wide, and Jordan was only pretending to be attracted to Margot, wasn't he?

A SEASON FOR CHANGE *by Margaret Way*
Samantha had never met anyone like Nico. He had everything and he was attracted to her. *So why was she so afraid of him?*

PERSONAL AFFAIR *by Flora Kidd*
Would it make the situation between Carl's cousin Greg and his fiancée Laura better, if Margaret tried to encourage Carl herself?

LOVE'S AGONY *by Violet Winspear*
Angie had hoped that Rique de Zaldo — now blind — would love her. But Rique was too bitter to care about any woman . . .

RYAN'S RETURN *by Lynsey Stevens*
The last thing Liv Denison wanted was her husband Ryan coming back to her. But deep inside her a tiny ember continued to glow . . .

If you have difficulty in obtaining any of these books from your local paperback retailer, write to:

Mills & Boon Reader Service
P.O. Box 236, Thornton Road, Croydon, Surrey, CR9 3RU.

Take romance with you on your holiday.

Holiday time is almost here again. So look out for the special Mills & Boon Holiday Reading Pack.* Four new romances by four favourite authors. Attractive, smart, easy to pack and only £3.00.

*Available from 12th June.

Dakota Dreamin'	**Forbidden Flame**
Janet Dailey	Anne Mather
Devil Lover	**Gold to Remember**
Carole Mortimer	Mary Wibberley

Mills & Boon
The rose of romance

SAVE TIME, TROUBLE & MONEY!
By joining the exciting NEW...

Mills & Boon

Romance CLUB

WITH all these **EXCLUSIVE BENEFITS** for every member

NOTHING TO PAY! MEMBERSHIP IS FREE TO REGULAR READERS!

IMAGINE the *pleasure* and *security* of having ALL your favourite *Mills & Boon* romantic fiction delivered right to *your* home, absolutely POST FREE... straight off the press! No waiting! No more disappointments! All this PLUS all the latest news of *new books* and *top-selling authors* in your own monthly MAGAZINE... PLUS *regular* big CASH SAVINGS... PLUS lots of wonderful strictly-limited, *members-only* SPECIAL OFFERS! All these exclusive benefits can be *yours* – right NOW – simply by joining the exciting NEW *Mills & Boon* ROMANCE CLUB. Complete and post the coupon below for FREE full-colour leaflet. It costs nothing. HURRY!

No obligation to join unless you wish!

FREE CLUB MAGAZINE Packed with *advance* news of latest titles and authors

Exciting offers of **FREE BOOKS** For club members ONLY

Lots of fabulous **BARGAIN OFFERS** —many at **BIG CASH SAVINGS**

FREE FULL-COLOUR LEAFLET!
CUT OUT CUT OUT COUPON BELOW AND POST IT TODAY!

To: MILLS & BOON READER SERVICE, P.O. Box No 236, Thornton Road, Croydon, Surrey CR9 3RU, England. WITHOUT OBLIGATION to join, please send me FREE details of the exciting NEW Mills & Boon ROMANCE CLUB and of all the exclusive benefits of membership.

Please write in BLOCK LETTERS below

NAME (Mrs/Miss) ....

ADDRESS ....

CITY/TOWN ....

COUNTY/COUNTRY...POST/ZIP CODE ....

Readers in South Africa and Zimbabwe please write to: P.O. BOX 1872, Johannesburg, 2000. S. Africa